Enslave

Also by Cathy Yardley

RAVISH
CRAVE

Enslave

Beauty Tames the Beast

Cathy Yardley

An Imprint of HarperCollinsPublishers

This book is a work of fiction. The characters, incidents, and dialogue are drawn from the author's imagination and are not to be construed as real. Any resemblance to actual events or persons, living or dead, is entirely coincidental.

HarperCollins books may be purchased for educational, business, or sales promotional use. For information please write: Special Markets Department, HarperCollins Publishers, 10 East 53rd Street, New York, NY 10022.

FIRST AVON RED PAPERBACK EDITION PUBLISHED 2009, REISSUED 2013.

Designed by Diahann Sturge

The Library of Congress has cataloged the original paperback edition as follows:
  Yardley, Cathy.
    Enslave / Cathy Yardley. — 1st Avon pbk. ed.
      p.   cm.
    ISBN 978-0-06-137609-2 (pbk.)
    I. Title.
  PS3625.A735E67   2009
  813'.6—dc22   2009012867

ISBN 978-0-06-226557-9

13   14   15   16   17   OV/RRD   10   9   8   7   6   5   4   3   2   1

To my writing support network:
Sylvia Mendoza, Cheryl Howe, Mary Leo,
Ara Hale Burklund, Lorelle Marinello, and all the
wonderful, crazy gals on the Duets loop. Thank you
for being there when I needed you, and helping me
get through 2008. I love you all.

Enslave

Chapter One

"My life is over!"

Nadia Bessonova tried not to roll her eyes as her youngest sister, Irina, wailed. She shot a quick glance at her elder sister, Jelena. Jelena was the picture of patient suffering, listening intently to Irina's tale of woe.

"It's been over a month," Jelena finally said, her voice soft and modulated. "It can't have gotten worse, Irina darling. We'll figure something out." She paused, then added hesitantly, "You might want to keep it down. Deidre is trying to get some sleep, and with the baby coming . . ."

Irina's nose wrinkled at the mention of their stepmother. "Always Deidre," she muttered. "Jelena, why can't I stay at your house? You've got more than enough room in that mansion." Irina cast an irritated glare at Nadia. "It's too crowded here. I can't turn around without tripping over someone, and forget about privacy. It's as bad as being back in the Ukraine."

"Hardly," Nadia said, her irritation rising. Irina had only been a child when they had truly hit rock bottom in the Ukraine. Nadia hadn't been that old, but she could still remember it clearly: the freezing cold, the packs of wild dogs roaming the streets. "Sharing a three-bedroom house in Las Vegas is better than sharing a single room in Kiev. It could be worse."

"Don't give me your 'we'll work through it, we'll survive it' speech, Nadia," Irina said sharply in Russian. "You're not the one whose wealthy husband just dumped her for an eighteen-year-old Chinese girl, fresh off the boat."

"He married you when you were an eighteen-year-old Russian girl," Nadia pointed out. "Really, how surprised could you have been?"

Irina yowled in protest, and Jelena stepped between them. "This is getting us nowhere," she said, her voice sharp and imperious as only extreme confrontation tended to bring out in her. "We need to focus. Thanks to Irina's prenuptial agreement, our family won't be getting the monthly stipend from him."

"Bastard didn't even let me take the jewelry to pawn," Irina muttered.

"So," Jelena continued practically, "we just need to figure out a way to make up the difference."

Nadia nodded, sighing. Especially with the baby on the way. The family survival depended on them.

Irina looked shrewd. "Maybe your husband, Jelena . . ."

Now it was Jelena's turn to sigh. "I will ask," she murmured. But the tension etched small lines at the corners of her eyes, making her look older.

"You just don't know how to handle him," Irina sniffed. "If he were my husband, I'd screw him like crazy until he'd do anything I wanted, then show him who was really boss in the household."

"If he was your husband," Nadia muttered, "he'd be changing the locks after picking up his mail-order bride catalog."

Irina glared.

"Nadia, how's father's import-export business doing?" Jelena asked, quickly changing the subject. "He acted like the caviar alone would make us some money."

"It's not going quite as well as we'd hoped," Nadia said, pushing aside the gnawing fear that had been eating at her for months. "But that's about to change, apparently. Papa said something about getting a big influx of money, by the end of the week."

"Really?" Irina looked hopeful. Nadia could almost see her developing a wish list in her head. Or, rather, a shopping list.

Jelena, on the other hand, narrowed her eyes suspiciously. "Did he say from where?"

"No."

Jelena's eyes widened. "He wouldn't," she breathed. "Not again."

"Of course not." Nadia fidgeted, wandering around the sparsely furnished living room. "He promised."

The doorbell rang.

The girls were on their feet. Jelena asked, glancing at her watch, "It's ten o'clock at night. Were either of you expecting anyone?"

Nadia's stomach clenched. Nothing good ever came from late-night visitors. Either it was "business associates" of her father's, who were angry about something, or police showing up to cart him off to jail. Neither choice was appealing.

He swore he'd stopped stealing cars, she thought despondently. *Why do we keep believing him?*

The doorbell rang again, insistent.

"I'll get it." Nadia strode to the front door, looking out the peephole as her heart started to hammer with dread. The outside light was broken: she could barely make out a looming shadow. She swallowed hard.

The doorbell rang a third time.

She went to the small table in the foyer, where she normally dropped her keys. Opening the drawer, she pulled out a Beretta nine-millimeter, holding it behind her back. Then she opened the door with her other hand, keeping the chain latched.

"Can I help you?"

The shadow was immense. His eyes gleamed, but everything else about him was masked in shadow. "I'm here to see Mikhail Bessonov." His voice was warm, deep and enveloping, like a mink fog.

"May I tell him who is here?"

"Tell him I'm the owner of the rose," he said. "He'll understand."

"If you could just wait here . . ." She knew it was rude, but she didn't know the man, and didn't trust his cryptic message. She shut the door, tucked the gun in the waistband of her jeans at the small of her back. Then she hurried to her father's bedroom, knocking softly.

Her father opened the door. At sixty, he still looked good—good enough to land her stepmother, who was only thirty. He was in pajamas, his reading glasses halfway down the bridge of his nose. "What is it?"

She glanced over. Deidre was asleep, the large bump of her pregnant belly protruding against the covers. "There's a man," she whispered. "He said he's the owner of the rose. He wants to talk to you."

"The rose?" Her father frowned with irritation. "What rose? What the . . ."

Then, suddenly, he went ghostly pale.

"Dear God," he breathed. "He's *here*? Already?"

"Papa, what is it?"

"Where?" Her father's voice shook. "Where is he?"

"I left him on the doorstep," she replied. "I . . ."

"We've got to get out of here," he said. "Are your sisters downstairs?"

"Yes," she replied, fear now flooding her bloodstream with adrenaline. "But . . ."

The doorbell rang again.

Her father rushed to his pregnant wife. "Deidre, wake up," he said, shaking her. "We've got to get out of here . . ."

There was the sound of a door crashing open. Deidre woke, startled. There was a scream. Nadia sprinted for the front door.

When she got there, she stopped. The man was standing there, beside the broken latch, in front of her sisters. Jelena and Irina cowered in the corner, holding each other, staring at the intruder. Nadia got a good look at him, and froze.

He was enormous. Easily six foot five, the man seemed to take up the entire foyer with his broad, muscular frame. Even in his tailored suit, there was something almost feral about him: an aura of leashed violence, just waiting to be released.

Then there was his face.

Angry red scars crisscrossed from his forehead, across his right eye, down the right side of his face, punctuated by a deep gash down his cheek. His eyes were a light, piercing color that seemed to hover between gray, then sea foam green, then a pale, clear blue. He stared back at her.

"Hasn't anyone told you staring isn't polite?"

His voice sent a shiver down her spine. He sounded urbane, sophisticated, bored. But there was anger beneath his words, a muted fury that singed her. She took an instinctive step back.

Her father hurried out in his pajamas. "I didn't know," her father said quickly, practically gibbering. She'd never seen him scared, not even when the Russian police had taken him to prison. "I swear to God, Roddy never told me who the car belonged to. Not until it was too late."

"Perhaps you should have done a little more research on your own. Besides, I've already had words with Roddy." The sentence, casually spoken, silenced her father immediately. Nadia sensed that the man had had more than "words" with her father's friend and fellow car thief, Roddy Templeton.

She wondered, abruptly, if Roddy was still alive.

"You got the car back, then?" her father said, his voice hoarse but hopeful.

"Unfortunately, no." Now the anger bubbled to the surface. "I hope you got a good deal of money, Mikhail, because that car was worth more to me than anything else I own." He paused. "It was certainly worth more to me than the life of a sniveling, stupid thief who chose the wrong man to fuck with."

The tension in the room nearly suffocated Nadia. This man was danger embodied. He wasn't here to chastise, or call the authorities. He was here to do some damage.

She couldn't allow this to happen.

She felt the cold steel of the gun barrel, nestled against her spine. Slowly, she reached behind her.

"Unless you're positive you can kill me before I can reach you," the man said, his eyes glowing, "think very carefully before you draw that gun."

Nadia paused, her hand in midair. She was a decent shot, and a nine-millimeter round was nothing to sneer at. But he was possibly too large for it to actually stop him. There was also the possibility she might miss.

She waited a long second. Then, slowly, she put her hand back down at her side.

He continued staring at her, as if sizing her up. His eyes gleamed, and his scars twisted. He seemed to be smirking.

"What are you going to do?" Nadia asked. "Kill him? Kill all of us? Over a car?"

He seemed surprised. Her father, on the other hand, was appalled. "Nadia!" he barked.

The man took a step closer to her, his presence overwhelming her senses. He stared down at her. "Don't I frighten you?"

"Does it matter?" she countered, not flinching, not even taking a step back, even though her neck craned painfully to look up into his eyes. "What do you want?"

"Nadia," her father hissed, stepping in front of her sisters, his eyes wild. "This is Dominic Luder. If you knew who he was . . . what he's capable of . . ."

"No, no," the man interrupted, without breaking eye contact with her. "In the first place, it wasn't simply a car. It was a 1958 Ferrari Testa Rossa, in its original red."

Testa Rossa. "Your rose," she whispered, stunned. That sort of a car was a collector's wet dream.

"Indeed," he admitted. "Do you know how much something like that costs?"

"Millions." She shot a quick, accusing glance at her father, who hung his head in shame.

"In the second place, it held a lot of, ah, *personal* meaning for me. It's going to be murder to get it back," the large man mused, and she wondered if he was being metaphorical. "You see why I'm so perturbed?"

"Perhaps I can steal it back," her father offered in a shaky voice. "Please. I'm sure we can work something out!"

"I'm not in the habit of negotiating," Dominic said, and slowly reached into his suit jacket. Impeccably tailored, the movement nevertheless revealed the telltale bulge of a gun. His eyes were a frozen, crystalline blue, like the sky in the Ukraine in December. He was going to do something terrible.

Unless she stopped him.

"What do you want?" she repeated, stepping between the giant and her father, her sisters. "If you kill him, or us, then you'll just be causing yourself more problems, and you still won't have your car. What would be the point?"

"Nadia!" This time, it was her sister Jelena who sounded horrified.

"Are you trying to get us killed?" Irina shrieked.

Nadia was waiting, trying to make sure he wasn't about to pull his gun. If he didn't kill her with the first shot, perhaps she could buy the others some time. Hopefully Deidre was out of the house. Should she try to shoot him? Or simply act as a shield? Her mind moved in the sped-up, hyper-clear mode that she shifted into when threatened. Quickly, efficiently, she cycled through possible scenarios.

She didn't have many options. What few choices she had were very, very bleak.

"You're either incredibly courageous, or astoundingly stupid," Dominic said, letting out a low, rumbling chuckle. "You really aren't afraid of me, are you?"

Something had changed in his eyes. She couldn't place it.

"I'm terrified of you," she said.

"But that hasn't stopped you."

She shook her head. "I'm not going to let you hurt my family," she said quietly. "Not without doing something. Anything."

"Nadia . . ." her father implored.

"Aren't you the brave one," the man said, with biting sarcasm. "What do you propose I do instead?"

Her mind whirred. She hadn't considered that he might be open to negotiation. New options clicked and shifted.

"Take me."

Everyone else in the room fell silent, and she felt them staring at her. She wasn't even sure where the idea came from.

Her mind flashed back, to a terrible afternoon in Chernihiv.

Sex is a universally accepted currency. The old doctor's horrible chuckle as he gave her an ultimatum: medicine in exchange for an hour on her back.

It hadn't been easy. But it needed to be done.

"You can keep me as collateral," she offered. "Until my father can get the car back. You can do whatever you want to me until then."

"Nadia, no," her father said, trying to pull her away. "Not this time! You don't understand . . ."

Dominic shot him a level stare, and her father's words stopped abruptly.

"Whatever I want, hmm?" Dominic's voice tickled over her nerve endings like a cloud. "Do you really know what that entails?"

She bit her lip as fear slashed at her heart.

"No," she admitted.

"But you'll still agree to it?" he asked. His voice sounded toneless, maybe casually curious. But the burning in his eyes suggested something else. "You'll do whatever I say? You'll keep your end of the bargain?"

She looked at her family—her terrified sisters, her parchment-pale father. Thought of her baby half-brother, still nestled in Deidre's womb.

It's temporary. You can survive it. For your family, you can do this.

She closed her eyes.

You always survive.

"Anything you want," she repeated, staring at Dominic solemnly.

His smile was fierce, the action pulling the scars of his face cruelly.

"Then we have a deal."

And without another word, he swept her up into his arms and carried her out of her father's house, into the Las Vegas night.

"What are we going to do?" Jelena asked her father, stunned, after Nadia disappeared.

Irina was crying, loud, dramatic sobs, until her father shocked them all by slapping her sharply across the face. Now, she stared at her father, petulant and afraid.

"Nadia has bought us some time," he said, and Jelena wasn't sure if he was convincing them, or himself. "She's done more than I ever could have asked."

"What are *we* going to do now?" Jelena clarified.

He stared at her with profound sadness. "What can we do?" he asked softly. "Your stepmother is pregnant. We have no money."

"You have the money from the stolen car," Jelena pointed out, wondering how much her father had made.

Was it worth it, compared to losing his daughter?

He shook his head. "I didn't make nearly as much as I should have—if I'd known who I was stealing from when I bargained the price . . . Besides, even if I gave him every dime I made, it'd be a drop in a bucket for a man like Dominic Luder. You heard him. The car is irreplaceable. We're only lucky he decided to . . ." He cleared his throat. "The best we can do is make sure your sister's sacrifice was not in vain."

Jelena gasped as the import of his melancholy words sank in. "You can't mean we're just going to let her stay with that man? Let him do . . ." She couldn't even begin to imagine what the frightening, scarred, vicious-looking man would do to her poor sister. "He could kill her!"

"You think I don't know that?" he yelled. Then a hopeful look crossed his face. "Your husband is rich. Perhaps he can help us."

Jelena blanched. "I can't ask," she said quickly. "Not for this. He'll tell me to go to the police."

"The police." Her father spat the words out. "We can't trust them. You know that."

He'd been in prison in Russia. They had not helped her family. She nodded, knowing his answer before she'd even finished her own sentence.

"We've got to get out of here," her father said instead. "It's not safe. He knows where we live. He could decide to come back anyway. We've got to protect the baby."

Irina looked nauseous. "He could come back?"

"You don't know what this man is capable of," her father said, and his voice actually trembled a little. "He's a legend.

He used to be on the West Coast somewhere, before a big mafia family in Las Vegas took him on. Killed his first man when he was seventeen, they say. Used to be really good-looking, I hear, but vicious. He was on his way to inheriting one of the biggest crime syndicates in Las Vegas. Then, once he got in that explosion . . ." He shuddered. "They say he's absolutely brutal now. They call him The Beast. There's an open contract out on his life, but he's like a ghost. No one can touch him. Anyone who crosses his path dies—or wishes he did."

Deidre was crying silently, her hand splayed over her large, protruding belly. Mikhail put a protective arm around his young wife.

"We've got to get out of here," Irina said, looking at Jelena now. "You've got to help us!"

Jelena sighed. "I will help you move. You'll stay in a hotel tonight."

"You will pay for that?" her father interjected.

Jelena felt a snap of anger. *You stole the fucking car. You're the reason we're in this mess. Why can't you pay for it?* "I'll pay for it."

Her unhappiness must have been obvious on her face. He took a step forward, his chin jutting forward defensively. "I was putting the car money aside, for an emergency, or for after the baby was born. I would think you'd want to help your family." He looked at her with reproach, and guilt burned in her chest like acid. "As your family has helped you."

"Of course, Papa," she said, bowing her head. "Let me make some calls."

"And talk to your husband," he added, straightening, looking more like the patriarch.

Jelena buried herself in the details of moving them out, gathering only essentials, leaving things behind. She'd been through this too many times before; it was a familiar routine. But her thoughts kept returning to Nadia. Nadia, whom she had resented for never being forced to marry, being their father's favorite.

Nadia, who she now realized had often disappeared just before their father had gained something of value. Nadia, who never complained, never asked for anything. Perhaps there was a different reason that Nadia was her father's favorite.

Jelena closed her eyes. Perhaps Nadia had not gotten the better end of the bargain, after all, in avoiding an arranged marriage.

"We must do something before that beast kills her," Jelena whispered, but no one in her scurrying family heard her.

I just thought you'd want to help your family . . .

It would be up to her, then. No matter what it took.

Nadia rode silently in the man's opulent car—a Maybach, unprepossessing but more expensive than most ostentatious luxury cars. The leather seats felt like butter against her skin; even the air was perfumed with expense.

Where is he taking me?

He obviously was very rich, and very dangerous. Even in the spacious car, he seemed to engulf the interior, forcing her to unconsciously scrunch against the door.

"Driving too fast for you?" he growled.

She jumped, suppressing a squeak. "No," she whispered.

"Then maybe you can let go of that handle."

She looked down to find herself white-knuckling the handle on the door. With effort, she forced herself to release it.

After an hour in the pitch-black desert, the environment changed. She could make out the silhouette of trees under the full moon. A forest? In Nevada?

They pulled off the interstate, going onto a gravel road, then a dirt one. Her heart beat quickly. Was he going to kill her, and leave her out for the animals in this godforsaken place? Somewhere no one would ever find her?

She didn't have anything that could be used as a weapon. She hadn't even brought her purse. Her gaze darted around the car: nothing she could use.

Oh, God. Oh, God.

She bit her lip, hard. The sharp pain forced back the beginning hyperventilation.

Focus, damn it. Panic solves nothing!

She was so intent on calming down that she didn't notice the looming gates until the car pulled easily onto the paved driveway. Lights flooded the vehicle, and she was momentarily blinded.

The gates swung open slowly, as if recognizing his car. He pulled up a long and winding drive until they reached a mansion. Her eyes widened as she took in the scope of it. More than a mansion. It was practically a palace, here in the middle of nowhere. A huge garage door swung open, revealing an immaculate, meticulously organized garage.

"Get out," he said, killing the engine and opening his door.

She opened the door and did as instructed, glancing around, still gauging options for potential weapons. If he was going to kill her, she wasn't going out without a fight.

He must have noticed her intention, because he smiled, causing the zipper of scarring across his face to ripple. "Most of the really heavy tools are in the cabinets, but there's a tire iron to your left, in that metal toolbox."

She glanced at the box. It was easily three feet away. A few steps, at best.

Before she could move, he was suddenly looming in front of her. How did someone so massive move so quickly, so quietly?

"I wouldn't, though." His light eyes gleamed, like fire trapped in ice. "If I were you."

She swallowed hard, and crossed her arms.

"Follow me."

She did, or tried. His long stride forced her to jog to keep up with him. He was moving quickly enough that she could barely get the details of the dimly lit house. The place was cavernous, comprised of dark woods and dark-tinted windows; jutting rock masonry, and the suggestion of shelves, although she couldn't make out what was on them. What in the world did a man like this display? Books? Artwork?

She blanched. Or did he show off a different type of trophy?

Her heart was racing and adrenaline flooded her system like poison. Tears stung at the corners of her eyes as she fol-

lowed him down a long hallway. He opened a dark mahogany
door, and turned on the lights.

"This will be your room."

She stepped inside, then paused, confused.

It was a lovely room—no, a lovely *suite*. It looked like something that would be offered in a luxury hotel on the Strip,
maybe something reserved for the biggest-spending high
rollers. There was a king-sized bed, dressed with a chocolate
brown and robin's egg blue comforter, surprisingly stylish.
On the wall, there was a large-screened plasma television.
There was even a large desk. Through the open door, she
could see a bathroom, complete with stall shower and deep,
sunken Jacuzzi tub. The only thing missing was a refrigerator and a personal safe. Maybe she hadn't seen them yet.

She glanced at him, puzzled. "Here? I stay . . . here?"

"I'd keep you in the garage, but the last girl I kept made a
terrible mess near my favorite car."

She gasped, taking a step back.

"For God's sake!" he exploded, and now she cowered.
"I'm not going to kill you, so stop cringing. I said, this is your
room. This is where you . . . you know, where you'll *sleep*."

Stay focused. She didn't know what his game was, but he
was scaring the hell out of her, and she was letting it engulf
her. No. She was here with a purpose. To save her family. If
she was lucky, to even remove a threat to her family.

She took a deep breath, and stepped silently across the
lush Berber carpet. "It's a nice room," she said, proud that
her voice held steady.

"Glad you approve." The sarcasm in his voice rasped at her.

Anger flashed momentarily, and she clung to it, grateful to displace the fear with any other emotion. "So if you're not going to kill me, what are you going to do to me?"

She forced herself to look squarely at him as she asked the question. In the gentle incandescent light, she could see him more clearly.

She'd already noticed his eyes, his scars. Now she took in the rest of him. He was tall, and built out of pure, solid muscle, draped in what surely was an expensive suit. His hair was shaggy, at odds with the careful details of his wardrobe; wavy and unruly, the long ends curled slightly over his collar. His longish bangs covered part of his face, she could tell. Perhaps deliberate?

No. She couldn't imagine this man trying to hide what he was from anyone.

He moved again, that quick, fluid movement, like a wolf. There was a wet bar, nestled into the wall; he poured himself something amber, a Scotch or a whiskey. "I don't know what I'm going to do with you," he admitted in a low voice, his back still turned to her.

She crossed her arms tightly against her chest. He couldn't possibly . . . was that remorse she heard in his voice?

"You're the one who said I could do whatever I wanted until your father returned my rose," he mused, and his tone was so bitter, she realized that she must be imagining the regret. "So perhaps you can tell me what you're planning to offer that can even begin to replace what I've lost."

It was like plunging into the frozen lakes back in the Ukraine—a shock so sharp it was numbing.

"Or I've got a better idea," he drawled, turning back to her. "Maybe you should show me."

"What do you want me to do?" she hedged, buying time.

He leaned against the bar, drink in hand, sardonic amusement etched on his face.

"You're the sacrificial maiden, here," he pointed out. "You're the noble one offering herself for her family. I'm just trying to figure out why, exactly, *taking* you was worth giving up vengeance against a man who stole the one thing in this world that meant anything to me."

Anger tinged his words again. He was starting to question their bargain, she realized, her palms sweating.

He was absolutely right in one thing: she'd made this bargain. If she was going to save her family, then she had to stop acting like a scared little mouse and get *on* with the thing, already.

He wanted sex. Didn't all men? So she'd give him that. It might be painful, but at least it wasn't difficult. She would get through it.

Without ceremony, she kicked off her shoes, then took off her clothes with clinical, detached speed. She tugged the sleeveless T-shirt over her head, then unzipped her loose-fitting jeans, dropping them to the ground. She peeled off her socks. She didn't look at him once, biting her lip as she reached behind her back to unclasp her plain pink cotton bra. She dropped it on the growing pile of clothes.

She made the mistake of looking up as she reached for the

waistband of her panties . . . white cotton, sprayed with violets, cut high on her thighs. The way he was looking at her made her pause.

He stared at her like a starving man. No, like a starving lion, something that wanted to pounce and devour her. The tension in his frame was palpable, even if he still stood, trying to seem bored, trying to seem removed from what was going on.

Slowly, she eased the panties down, past her thighs, down her legs. His eyes followed her every movement, until she was finally completely naked, standing in the middle of the room. She stood, awkward, unsure of what to do next.

He wasn't bored. He put his glass down on the counter blindly, close to the edge, and pushed away from the wet bar. He took a step toward her, and it was all she could do to stand her ground. She lifted her chin instead, challenging him.

Here I am. Take me.

He circled her, reminding her again of some fierce, feral animal. But he kept his distance as he looked at her, she noticed. He was wary. Wary of her, the naked and defenseless one.

She frowned. Why in the world would *he* be cautious?

She felt the heat from his hand, close to her body—but not quite touching her. Her skin burst out in goose bumps that had nothing to do with the slight hum of the air conditioner, chilling the room. His hand grazed her hip, her shoulder; she felt the warmth against her hair, felt it shift slightly. He stood behind her, his looming presence like a blanket, smothering her. She heard him take in a deep, slightly shuddering breath.

Was he . . . *smelling* her?

She turned to face him, ready to yell at him to just take her already and stop tormenting her. She turned so quickly that she caught the unguarded expression on his face.

His blue eyes were vulnerable—as if his interest in her was helpless, compelled. There was something about his face that seemed both hopeful and despairing. He wanted her, but it wasn't just a carnal desire. Whatever he wanted from her, he wasn't about to simply reach out and take, even though she was standing there like an unwrapped Christmas present. It was as if he were afraid to touch her.

His look was one of mute anguish, pleading for understanding. It was so gentle and at odds with the rest of him— his huge, fearsome body; his scarred, brutal face—that she felt her heart ache, for a split second.

He leaned closer to her, to her face, as if he were going to kiss her neck. He hovered there, and she felt the heat coming off his body, like a bonfire.

She bridged the gap. Her hand went up slowly, cupping his face, feeling the hardened ridges of scar tissue beneath her fingertips.

He swept her up in a lightning fast movement that had her head swimming. In the next second, it seemed, they were on the bed. He was kissing her, all but devouring her. She couldn't get her bearings, couldn't register any sensations beyond the ones that he was submerging her in.

She surfaced for air as he stripped off his luxurious suit with obvious, growling impatience. It was as if a dam had burst, and he was all but exploding through his civil façade.

He stretched out next to her, covering her. She felt a moment's fear, but it was dwarfed by the sheer feel of being overwhelmed by him. He had more scars: his chest was hatch-marked with them; she could feel the roughness of them against her chest, dragging against her nipples. But before she could do more than gasp, he was kissing her again, focusing on her mouth, his lips caressing hers—yes, the soft, gliding movements were definitely caresses, she thought, before his hand cupped her breast in a manner that startled her with its tender firmness. His tongue tickled at the sensitive inner flesh of her lips, not invading but coaxing. Tempting.

She would have remained frozen, but her body was responding in a way that was entirely unfamiliar to her. She didn't know how to move, but he was somehow drawing the response from her, causing her hips to rise fractionally to meet the hard, hot length of his erection, pressed like a branding iron against her inner thigh. She opened her mouth wider, perhaps to breathe, but his tongue swept in, capturing hers, taunting it. She was kissing him before she realized what she was doing. She heard a moan, too high to be masculine.

She was moaning, she realized. She was gasping, moaning beneath his fingertips. He played her like a violin, and her body sang.

She could feel the ridges of his scars against her neck as he suckled her throat, her collar bone, her shoulder. She shivered and cried out as he reached lower, between their bodies, reaching right for her heat. It was a shock, and she winced, making him pause ever so slightly. His fingers didn't thrust inside her, though. Instead, they stroked, rubbing at her clit, gently penetrating her curls, nuzzling between the folds of skin until he found her quickly hardening nubbin. She found her hips bucking against his fingertips as he maneuvered against her, the dampness of his cock dragging against her flesh echoed in the surprisingly swift rush of her own wetness. When his thick fingertips finally pushed inside her, her body was more than ready for the onslaught. He delved deep, stroking inside her, still rubbing her clit with his thumb.

She was close to orgasm, her breathing rushed and ragged. Her mind felt wild, overwhelmed.

He maneuvered his wide hips between her thighs, covering her like a huge blanket, enveloping her with his heat. She closed her eyes, trying to process everything, feeling powerless but at the same time swept up in it; not drowning, but instead riding an incredible wave, letting it carry her of its own volition . . .

When he plunged inside her, she gasped loudly. His cock was enormous, and the pain of his entry was momentarily shocking.

He froze, and she heard his muttered cursing. She felt bereft. Then, slowly, he moved, his hips gracefully pressing against hers, the feel of his body pushing against her clit helping ease the transition. Her body stretched, accommodating him. The pain ebbed.

He reached between them again, even as his mouth claimed hers. The kiss wasn't invasive; rather, it was tender, perhaps even apologetic.

She wasn't sure when she started kissing back, only that it felt natural to do so.

He withdrew by an inch, then pressed forward. Repeated the action, gently, without causing pain. Slowly, maddeningly slowly, he would withdraw further and then delve deeper, his body rocking against hers.

The pressure was building again. She could feel it, the creeping edge of orgasm that had been hinted at earlier haunting her, moving closer, dancing across every nerve ending. She found her hips rising up to meet his, felt her thighs pressing tightly against his pelvic bones as her breasts dragged against his scars. She gripped his shoulders loosely, biting her lip.

He breathed harder, growling against her. It was like holding a wolf, huge and untamed. But she didn't care. The wildness that was building inside her answered the animal call.

The orgasm finally exploded inside her, and she cried out, her body hugging his penis in hard, drawing waves. Suddenly he was slamming against her rippling body, his cock surging inside her, his hips rolling against her in quick, pumping bursts. He snarled in defiance, a loud shout as his cock jerked and erupted in her. She could feel every jolt of his release, a hard push against the secret spot inside her. Her orgasm, which had been rippling softly into after-shocks, burst back into glowing life, and she screamed in pleasure, her pussy clenching around him like a fist.

Afterward, he rolled to the side, still buried inside her. She felt dazed, as if the whole thing were too surreal to have actually happened. She turned to look at him. His face looked more placid than she would have imagined, his eyes closed.

She reached for him, her fingertips just brushing the side of his face.

His eyes flew open, and he jerked back, his body disengaging from hers. He moved off the bed, glaring at her, magnificent and huge in his nudity. Even his scars, though menacing, only seemed to add to the overall impression: fierce. Warrior. Dangerous.

Impressive.

His voice was loud, harsh. "You said I can do whatever I want with you," he snapped. "You brokered this deal. This is your life now. This house is your prison." He scooped up the clothes on the floor, hers as well as his. "You'll be naked. I will see you whenever I want. *Touch* you whenever I want. You'll do whatever I say."

"Y-Yes," she stammered.

He leaned over her, moving close, and she could feel the heat of his breath, warming her jaw, her neck.

"You'll regret the day you told me to take you." His voice was like broken glass. "God help you, we both will."

With one last searing look, he got up, leaving the room, slamming the door behind him.

She lay back on the bed, stunned. Why was he so angry, she panicked. What had she done wrong?

And what was she going to do now?

Chapter Two

Twelve-thirty that night, Jelena's husband, Henry, still wasn't home yet. That wasn't unusual; he often socialized without her, and she never complained. Instead, she waited, ready to fix the bedtime Scotch-and-soda that he liked, the bed turned down, wearing her prettiest smile. So far, it had all worked beautifully. She knew it didn't pay to rock the boat. It was why she was still his wife, even after six years since he'd requested her from the bride catalog. He could easily find a replacement for her in those same pages—just as Irina's husband had, presumably.

Oh, but I'll be rocking the boat tonight with this news.

Her family had sacrificed a lot to get her in this position. English lessons, special diet, special clothes and makeup. She'd even gone to one of those classes in Moscow, the one that taught you how to please a rich husband, with everything from how to stand to how to increase the pressure between your thighs. Since getting married, she'd learned how to be on committees and how to socialize with his high-powered associates and their wives. She'd never questioned Henry, never embarrassed him, never did anything she thought might remotely anger him. In return, he'd given her a generous spending account, and he'd given her family a healthy stipend to live on once he'd brought them over from Moscow. He showed her off, and she'd done her best to compliment him. He'd even shown her some tenderness.

She heard his footsteps, coming down the hallway, and she smoothed down the sexy white lingerie he'd bought her for Valentine's Day.

Sex usually helped when she needed something. She needed all the help she could get.

She smiled as best she could as he walked through the door of the bedroom suite. "Henry," she murmured, pouring his drink.

"That's my girl," he said, barely looking at her as he took the drink. He started taking off his tie, looking tired. Old.

This was a bad time to ask. Were it anything else, she'd table the issue until the morning. But it was too important. It couldn't wait.

He seemed to sense her unease, finally, looking at her quizzically. "Jelena?"

"How was your day?" she hedged.

"The same." He took a long pull from the square-cut glass. "Knocking around assholes at work, getting things done.

And a business meeting tonight, so I have to act happy while those young jackals get plowed on my expense account."

She wasn't quite sure what exactly it was he did at work, but it seemed he was crucial. She knew he dealt with a lot of stress. "Did you want me to give you a massage?"

"Not tonight, Lena," he said. "I just want to go to bed."

She took a deep breath, her heart beating rapidly. "I need to talk to you."

He'd been heading for the closet, his shirt halfway off his shoulders. His hands paused, glancing at her. "About what?"

"My family," she said slowly. "My sister. She's in trouble."

He grimaced, removing his shirt the rest of the way and throwing it on the floor, even though the hamper was a mere foot away. "Your family's in trouble. I might've guessed," he said, and for a second she hated him. Hated to ask for his help. Hated having him there at all. "What, is Irina pregnant?"

"No."

"Nadia, then?" He looked like he'd eaten a lemon.

"Yes," she said carefully, her palms sweating. "I mean, she's not pregnant. It's . . ."

"Don't tell me. She's finally met somebody, and they need money for a wedding?"

"No." How was she going to broach this? Her tongue felt like lead in her mouth.

His eyes narrowed as he loosened his pants, letting them fall to the floor as well. "Wait a minute. Is this related in any way to your father's little sideline *business* ventures? The kind that landed him in the Gulag back in the old country?"

She didn't answer. She didn't have to.

"No. Absolutely not." She could see the tension coil through his body. "I told you when we got married, Jelena. I'll give them money every month, but I don't want to have anything to do with your Dad's criminal activities. I can't afford to have that kind of shit attached to me. You *know* that."

She cringed. "But . . . but Nadia . . ."

"I don't care if they're calling it import-export, I'll bet that she helps him steal those fucking cars," he muttered. "You'd have been better off leaving the bunch of 'em back in Moscow."

"They're family," she lashed out, with more venom than she'd ever displayed. "My father made sure we survived. Without family loyalty, *we have nothing.*"

Henry started to say something, then obviously thought the better of it, looking at her face.

"Look, Jelena, I know how much your family means to you, but I'm not going to dig them out of a hole I'm sure they got themselves into," he said, and he was so patronizing about it—she wanted to slap his face. "Maybe, I'll increase their stipend, okay? Another hundred bucks, yeah. Okay, two. But I can't do more than that, and I don't want you to ask me to. Not ever again." His voice was firm.

"It's more serious than that," she said. "Nadia's with this man, this horrible man . . ."

"What, did he drag her off?" Henry said, looking skeptical.

She bit her lip. "Sort of . . ."

Henry's cruel laugh cut her off. "Jesus. Another deal. Hey,

it worked fine for you, right? You're lucky you got me. Don't worry. He'll probably trade her in after a few years. She's a tough kid."

"You know people. You've got connections," she pleaded, desperation clawing at her. "You could help her!"

He frowned, as if he couldn't believe she'd continued talking, against his express wishes. "I said *no*, Jelena. That's final."

With that, he retreated into the bedroom.

I've done everything you've ever asked me. I'm the perfect wife. I would be the perfect mother if you'd let me have children.

Anger, dark and viscous, bubbled through her.

I earned my family's money.

She followed him silently into the bedroom. He was down to just boxers and socks. He still had a nice physique, considering being somewhere in his fifties and having a high-stress desk job. He still had his hair. He put his glasses down on the nightstand, finishing the last of his Scotch with a flourish. She floated beside him, barely dipping the mattress as she got on her side of the bed.

He shut the light out, plunging her into darkness.

She'd learned to love him, strangely enough. At least, she'd thought she loved him. But she'd married him because he promised her he'd get her family out of Russia, away from the theft, and the dogs, and the crushing poverty. She'd done what her family required, and she continued to go through with it.

For my family . . .

She felt Henry's hand on her shoulder, stroking it perfunctorily before reaching down to cup her breast.

"Come on," he murmured, and the scent of alcohol permeated him. "You wore my favorite lingerie. No sense wasting it, right?"

Instead, she turned away from him.

He growled. "Like that, huh? You don't get what you want, you think you can cut me off?"

She never had before. She felt her stomach knot.

"Well, then, *fuck you* Miss High-and-Mighty!" His voice was disembodied in the darkness, like an angry ghost. "If this is the way you're going to be, maybe I need to rethink *our* little *contract*, huh?"

And with that parting shot, she felt the bed creak as he turned his back on her.

She swallowed hard, feeling tears edge out from the corners of her eyes. She knew that he didn't love her, not the way she'd read about in romance novels. But she thought he'd at least be someone she could turn to for help. Someone who might understand. But no, now he was acting like a spoiled child. Or, worse, treating *her* like a spoiled child.

In the meantime, her sister was in the hands of a madman who might be torturing her as Jelena lay there, on her thousand-count Egyptian cotton sheets, next to the man she'd been sold to.

Jelena winced. Dear God, compared to Nadia, her years of marriage were a fantasy of comfort. Nadia, who had never been offered in marriage. Still, she must have been "offered" in the short term, hadn't she? Nadia didn't have Jelena's stunning, angelic beauty, or Irina's voluptuous sex appeal. Many had said that Nadia was the most unconventionally beautiful, the one that looked the most like their mother, with her mink brown hair and large, dark eyes. Nadia was the one that stayed home, helped the family. Jelena had resented Nadia for her "easy" life.

Looking back, perhaps her sister wasn't so lucky after all.

Jelena frowned as Henry started to snore loudly. He was going to replace her soon: she wasn't blind, wasn't stupid. Another time, this might have filled her with some dread. Would she be able to find another husband, one that would replace her family's lost income? Would she still fulfill her responsibilities? Or, worse, had she done something so wrong that another man wouldn't want her?

That wasn't her fear tonight. Her whole life seemed to focus on one thing: rescuing Nadia. Or punishing the man who had condemned her to her fate.

If Henry wouldn't help her . . . then by God, she would find someone who would.

Nadia woke in the darkness with a gasp, her heart hammering as she faced complete disorientation.

What happened? Where am I?

Then her mind filled in the details.

Dominic Luder. The bargain.

Last night . . .

She must have fallen asleep. She reached blindly for a light, fumbling until she managed to turn on the bedside lamp. The room was as she remembered it: gorgeous, subtly masculine.

Apparently impossible to escape from. She frowned. After he'd left, she'd tried the windows—they were hermetically sealed, some kind of unbreakable glass. At least, it hadn't managed to shatter based on whatever she'd tried smacking against it. And he'd locked her in for the night, too.

What does he want from me?

He'd been mocking, angry—at himself or her, she couldn't quite tell. Probably both. But he was honoring the terms of the agreement, so far. He was keeping her. As far as she could tell, he had no further interest in harming her family.

You will regret the day you told me to take you.

She'd never seen a man so furious. So dangerous. So passionate . . .

She clenched her hands into fists, feeling a helpless anger overtake her. If only she could figure out what the hell he wanted from her!

She needed to get her bearings, and figure out either how to escape, or how to ensure her family's safety . . . whether that meant pleasing him, or killing him and removing the threat. She stepped into the bathroom. It was every bit as sumptuous as the rest of the suite, with a large marble tub and a glass-enclosed stall shower. "If this is the guest room, what is the master bath like?" she whispered, turning on the water. She stepped inside, letting the warm water pulse over her naked flesh. It felt like heaven, and for a moment, she closed her eyes, letting it massage her. There were several nozzles, and it caressed her entirely. The hot, wet pressure reminded her of Dominic.

Suddenly dizzy, she put her palm flat on the wall for balance, resting her forehead against the cool tiles. The way he had looked at her was more profound than ways other men had touched her. And when he'd touched her . . .

She shivered, remembering.

The men she'd bargained with, in the past, had only cared about their own pleasure. The old doctor was aroused by her revulsion, by the fact that he could force her to his will; the *Bratva* mobster who her father had mistakenly double-crossed had also found her reticence enticing. The international visa agent who helped send her family to the United States had been American, and much more gentle—he'd actually taken some finessing. Still, he'd overlooked her lackluster performance, assuming that he was in fact an excellent lover and that her overdramatic cries of passion were real.

Her few lovers had meant well, but by that time she'd been too used to playing a role to insist on her own enjoyment. She couldn't get out of her head. They were usually done before she could manage an orgasm of her own, and she didn't mind. In fact, she encouraged their speed. She frowned. That was probably why no one had touched her in a year.

She smoothed her hands down the wet-slick planes of her body. Remembering his hands on her. His mouth.

Her body tingled, making the hot water seem cool compared to her suddenly feverish flesh. Her stomach clenched, and her hand closed over her breasts, then lower, her fingertips hovering over the sensitive flesh between her thighs. The way he'd stroked her, bringing her to a frenzy . . . she bit her lip against a silent moan of remembrance.

He threatened to kill your family.

Her hand dropped away, and she felt a surge of nauseous guilt. She reached out, turning the water's spray to cold. The icy droplets felt like slaps of punishment for her traitorous thoughts. When she got herself under control, she got out of the shower shivering, and wrapped herself in one of the thick Turkish-cotton towels.

It was as close to clothing as she was going to get. Making a makeshift sarong, she headed for the door, trying the handle gingerly. To her surprise, it was unlocked.

She stepped out into a long hallway. There were doors all around her, including one at the end of the hallway. She needed to find an exit, not another room. She headed for the open end. The lower ceiling opened to a cathedral-vaulted living room, replete with a huge gray-slate fireplace and a latticework of large, sturdy wooden beams. It looked architectural, simple, clean. Masculine, like her suite, yet subtly artistic.

Obviously, he'd lavished a lot of time and money on this place. Or someone had.

He's not going to just let you waltz out of here. He wants something. Find out what he wants.

He'd enjoyed the sex—then he'd gotten angry. Why? She couldn't remember doing anything wrong . . . except maybe enjoying it. She felt a blush blossom over her face, down her throat, across her exposed chest.

She'd touched him, she remembered.

No. *She'd touched his scars.*

Her eyes narrowed. His appearance. He'd made oblique comments about it before. He obviously had problems with it. But he'd enjoyed the sex with her, enough to let his guard down. She'd just have to seduce him—see if she could get him to forget about his disfigurement for a while. Personally, she didn't think his looks were so horrible, especially once she got used to it.

Of course, he could look like an ogre: the way he'd touched her, kissed her . . .

"I told you to be naked."

She gasped, spinning toward the deep voice behind her. She bumped into Dominic. How could he be so damned silent?

He reached out, his knuckles grazing her breasts as he released the tucked end of the towel. The cloth pooled at her feet, and for a moment she fought the urge to cover herself with her hands. Instead, she stared up at him, directly into his eyes. They were more gray than blue this morning. If, presumably, it was morning. Apparently the man did not believe in clocks.

"That's better," he said, and his eyes blazed as he surveyed her, starting with her feet and moving slowly upward. She could feel his stare like a velvet glove, smoothing over her flesh. Her nipples tightened as his gaze lingered there for a long moment. His eyes widened in response.

"What do you want from me?" she asked, then bit her lip. She'd meant to ask something more submissive and coaxing—*what can I do for you?* But he'd caught her off guard, and the question came out defensive.

He smiled at her coldly. "What've you got?"

He'd been like this last night, she remembered, only less playful. Then, he'd wanted her to convince him. Admittedly, her attempt at seduction had been derailed by her fear and indecision. Nevertheless, he'd responded.

She should try to seduce him now, she realized. See what he did when she had her wits about her.

She stepped forward boldly, arching her back slightly, letting her breasts jut forward. Her eyes never left his as she put one foot forward, then the other, until she was almost touching him. She could feel his warm breath on her face.

Then, without warning, her stomach yowled.

She felt her cheeks flush, and she quickly bit her lip and looked away. *Oh, yeah. That's seductive, you idiot.*

He actually let out a burst of surprised laughter. "Maybe you should show me what you're capable of after you've had something to eat," he said, amusement lacing every word.

She shrugged, embarrassment broiling her.

"Come on. Let's get you fed," he said, gesturing to her to follow him.

She strode next to him, marveling internally at the length of his strides. He really was enormous.

Her mind flashed to the thought of him buried inside her, and she squirmed as an unwelcome bolt of pleasure shot through her. *Enormous.* Her thighs pressed together, and she bit her lip.

He led her to the kitchen. "Have a seat there, at the counter," he instructed, "and I'll cook up something."

"You cook?"

His scar puckered as he sent her a half-smile. "I have a few skills, yes."

She lifted herself onto the high barstool, embarrassed by the feel of the cold wood against her bare buttocks. After a few moments, she forgot about her wariness and her desire to escape as she watched him fetch ingredients from the refrigerator, assembling them on the countertop. Fresh vegetables with vibrant colors, slices of tissue-thin meat, an assortment of cheeses, nuts, fruits. He assembled a surprisingly artistic tray.

"Nothing fancy, I'm afraid," he said critically. "We'll do better at dinner."

"If I didn't watch you, I would've sworn you had this tray catered." She bit her lip. "You don't have a chef, then? Or a personal cook?" *Or someone else that might help me escape?*

"I have some people who help on occasion, but you'll never meet them. They get paid very, very well to insure they don't invade my privacy. And they know me well enough not to try delving into places they're not welcome."

So much for that possibility. She shifted her weight, feeling awkward. There was a kitchen table . . . maybe that would be a better option, making her feel less on display. She started to get down from the barstool, but he shook his head. "We'll eat here," he instructed.

Still, he didn't sit next to her. He stood by her chair, putting the tray in front of her. Then he turned the chair slightly, so she was facing him, the tray to her left. The buckle of his leather belt brushed against her knees.

"Don't you want to sit?" she asked, her voice trembling slightly as her heart started to speed up. From this proximity, she could smell the subtle mix of his expensive cologne and the woodsy, masculine scent that was his alone.

He shook his head. "I think I'll feed you, Nadia."

"I can feed myself."

He stared at her, long enough, silently enough to make her shift her weight, crossing her arms in front of her chest again. "Whatever I want, Nadia," he reminded her, in a low voice.

"If you insist," she breathed.

"Graciously done," he said, his voice faintly mocking. He selected a cube of cheese. "I think you'll like this. It's a Basque goat cheese, with just a hint of nutty flavor. Can you tell?"

He popped the morsel into her mouth. She chewed slowly, confused. What *was* he playing at? Was he trying to make her feel comfortable, or uncomfortable?

Either way, it was working. The heat from his body reminded her of the pleasures of the previous night. She could feel her nipples puckering, and her heart was beating like a hummingbird's with every delectable bite. Lust warred with guilt and nerves. *What does he want from me?*

She swallowed hard. "It's good," she admitted, even though enjoying the food was the furthest thing from her mind.

"Even better with this," he said, breaking off a piece of rough bread. "This is cabernet walnut bread."

He fed her slowly, encouraging her to savor every bite. He

kept up a running commentary: this was obviously a man who loved food. It seemed as if he was more interested in the descriptions of each course than in whom he was feeding it to. Or at least, it would have seemed that way, if he didn't stroke her bottom lip as he placed some of the food in her mouth . . . or the way he made her lean forward, her mouth open, to retrieve some of the bites. He didn't even let her help with her hands, forcing her to nibble out of his palm on several occasions. When her teeth grazed the pad of his thumb, she thought she saw him shudder slightly.

She was getting damp, between her legs. She shifted her weight on the chair, trying not to think of the fact that all he needed to do was undo his buckle, his fly, and he'd be right there, at practically the right height . . .

She knew, as a seductress, perhaps she ought to reach for him. Undo his pants herself. But her nerve abandoned her, and she simply found herself eating and second-guessing herself.

By the time he suggested dessert, she felt full, but the promise of something sweet was seductive to her fully-awake taste buds. She'd never been so aware of different flavors and textures as she was at this one "casual" meal.

"You strike me as a woman who appreciates a decadent dessert," he said. "Have you ever had chocolate-covered cherries?"

"Of course," she said. Irina loved American candy: her now ex-husband had delivered boxes and boxes of the stuff when they were still negotiating the marriage, all varieties of candies, and Irina had often shared. "I find most of them too sweet, though."

"You'll like these, I think," he said, producing a plate. There were cherries on the stem, so dark they were a plump purplish-black, their color blending into the rich dark chocolate swirled around each end. He held one up by the stem. "Open wide, Nadia."

She did without thinking, tilting her head back, her tongue darting out to guide the fruit between her lips. She bit down, and the cherry flavor exploded in her mouth, sweet and tart and brilliant, the dark chocolate slowly mingling in a seductive counterpoint. She sighed with pleasure, closing her eyes.

"Another?"

She opened her eyes to find him staring at her, his expression almost predatory. He held up another cherry. She smiled, tilting her head back.

This time, when she bit down, he leaned forward, his hot lips brushing against the pulsing vein in her neck . . . at the same time his fingers pressed between her thighs, one fingertip delving inside her moist curls, brushing against her clit.

She almost choked. The vibrancy of the flavors, and the startling heated pleasure of his touch caused her to moan, her senses momentarily overwhelmed.

He smiled, a mysterious wizard's smile. "Another?" he asked casually, as if he had never touched her.

She blinked at him, unsure of what to do or say. Was he referring to the cherry? Or . . . the other?

"I . . ." She felt completely unfocused, helpless.

"Not sure, hmmm?" A tinge of laughter in his voice, even as the heat in his eyes didn't back down one degree. His finger traced and explored, and she gasped, scooting slightly toward him, making a strangled little cry in her throat.

"Dominic . . ."

Abruptly, he pulled his hand away. She couldn't help it: she whimpered.

"Like I said," he grinned wickedly. "Dinner will be better."

He left the tray, then walked out of the kitchen. She waited, unsure of what he was going to do.

After five minutes, she realized: he wasn't coming back.

She rubbed her arms, feeling goose bumps beneath her fingertips. She was supposed to be seducing *him*, not the other way around. And why was he bothering, anyway, when he'd made it quite clear he owned her? And if he wanted to seduce her, why hadn't he taken it all the way? Why had he turned her on like a blowtorch, then left her to smolder alone?

She was staring around the kitchen, trying to make sense of what had happened, when her eyes lit on an object on the counter that he'd forgotten to put away.

There, on the cutting board, was a small, sharp knife.

Chapter Three

Several hours later Dominic walked toward the guest suite, nerves jangling. It had been a while since he'd been with a woman. He paused, his hand on the doorknob.

Before *last* night, he corrected, it had been a while since he'd been with a woman.

He hadn't meant to sleep with her when he brought her home. He was surprised that he'd even gotten her into his car, and he'd berated himself the whole way back, but he couldn't bring himself to turn around and return her and extract his vengeance—probably because it would have been in front of her.

She really believed it, the whole nine yards: she was a noble sacrifice. She was saving her family. She was embracing the beast in order to rescue the ones she loved. In the old Greek plays, she'd be Iphigenia, the daughter of the king, going bravely to her death to save the world.

He hated that fucking play.

But once she'd gotten naked, his body had reacted. She was perfection. Not the plastic, Las Vegas fabricated version of perfection: she was beautiful, subtle, innocent. She wasn't acting out the drama. She had a job to do: she was doing it.

Part of him wanted to break her for it, he knew that. But that wasn't the part that had been released when he'd touched her. When he'd touched her, he felt a sort of reverence he hadn't felt in years. Maybe ever.

She was genuinely good, and he had no rights to her.

So why are you doing this?

He pulled away from the door, frowning at himself. Second-guesses weren't in his repertoire. Neither were regrets, come to that. And then there was his little seduction scene in the kitchen. He knew that she was going to try and play him—act like a coy mistress, drive him crazy. But he wasn't always this misshapen monster. He hadn't used those skills in years. It was amazing that they'd come back at all, much less as easily—he found himself falling into the old role.

Why was he doing this anyway?

Because he wanted her. Because she'd made this deal, not he. If you made a bargain, you paid for it with your soul. One way or another.

He stepped inside the room.

It was dark already, and from the light spilling in from the hallway, he could see that she was already in bed. Was she that eager, he wondered? Even as a touch of smug satisfaction pulsed through him, his subconscious was already sensing something amiss.

He took her for more of a fighter than that. Even if she did like having sex with him—and he got the feeling she'd had precious little enjoyable sex in her life—would she really be waiting for him like this?

He took off his clothes, quickly, methodically, trying to temper his impatience. He slid between the cool sheets, reaching for her. His hands grazed over the silky softness of her bare skin. For a moment, he explored her with his fingertips, enjoying the curves and plains of her body with a silent sigh. She felt incredible. Her breasts weren't large, but they were round and high, full enough to meet his cupped palms. Her waist was small, flaring out into delightfully curved hips and that sweet ass that begged for the touch of his hands. Even her limbs were long and lithe, dancer's limbs. His cock tightened painfully.

"Let's consider this dinner," he murmured, pressing hot, random kisses across her torso. She didn't answer. Her body was tense, but it wasn't the tension he was expecting.

Immediately, his mind went on alert.

She's up to something.

He felt what should have been a coaxing smile tug at the scar tissue crossing his cheek. "Come on, Nadia," he whispered, trying to trick her, get her guard down. "Tell me what you want."

Her body was stiff as a plank, and her breathing was fast. Too fast.

She wasn't turned on. *She was scared.*

He pulled away from her, and she murmured some incoherent sound of protest as she drew him closer.

She had never been frightened of him, not really, and he wouldn't see why that would have changed in the few hours since lunch, when she looked like she wanted to slip his cock inside her herself. Unless . . .

Unless she were a better actress than he'd given her credit for. Unless he had grossly misjudged her. Maybe now she was finally letting her fear catch up with her, and she could no longer hide her repugnance for what she was being forced to do.

Pain lanced through him. *How many times are you going to let some beautiful woman play you?*

He growled, reaching for the light, turning it on. She was pale, her eyes huge. Her hands were under the pillow, behind her head. She stared at him with obvious fear.

"Going back on your word, are you?" Anger and self-recrimination made his words acidic. "Anything I want, whenever I want. Your fucking bargain."

"You can have me," she protested weakly. Her pulse was beating like a hummingbird's wings against the ivory skin in the column of her neck.

"Last night, you were a much better actress," he mocked. "Lose your motivation?"

She stiffened as if he'd slapped her. She didn't meet his gaze. "I enjoyed last night. I wasn't pretending."

"Obviously." He started to roll away from her. "You don't seem to care about your family very much, if this is . . ."

She stopped him by grabbing his hand. Before he could tug

it away, she spread her legs, guiding his hand there, pressing his fingers into her pussy.

He stared at her, confused. She was already wet.

"What have you been doing?"

"Waiting for you." She still didn't look at him. She sounded miserable.

Just waiting for him had gotten her like this? He wanted to believe her, desperately. He stroked his fingers, feeling her slick skin, watching as she bit her lower lip, her hips moving incrementally to better accommodate him. "Then why, Nadia? Why do you seem so scared?"

"If I do anything wrong . . . if I don't *please* you . . . then you'll kill me, and them. Right?" She finally met his gaze. There was still something wrong. Well, obviously wrong, but there was something *off* about her anger. "So why shouldn't I be scared?"

He leaned forward, his fingers tracing her delicate skin, finding the erect triangular bump of her clit. "Then what about this?" He stroked it firmly, circling it and the flesh around it.

Her eyes closed and her head tilted back helplessly. "That's . . . just . . . oh, God . . ."

He smiled, relief flooding his system. It wasn't that she was scared of him. She was scared of how he was making her feel.

He wanted to roar. He suddenly felt like a god, lust and power and a sense of invincibility roaring through him like a drug. "Tell me if you still feel scared after this," he murmured, moving between her thighs. His head dipped down, his hands splaying her cunt, leaving her displayed like a banquet. Eagerly, he devoured her.

She let out a short shriek of surprise, then a long, low moan as his mouth closed over her clit, grazing it with his teeth, his tongue exploring her salty flesh thoroughly and insistently. He felt her hips rise from the bed, felt her swivel to change the pressure of his intimate kiss. He angled his head, his tongue lapping at her, moving lower to the well of her folds, her very entrance. He tasted a rush of wetness. *Citrus,* he thought, *mixed with the spicy tang that was purely her.* His tongue delved deeper, penetrating her. He felt her thighs clamped against his head, and another wave of wetness bathed his senses.

"Dominic," she gasped, her hips moving spasmodically. "Oh, Dominic."

He gripped her clenched buttocks, pulling her hard against him, fucking her with his tongue as his cock clenched and ached with jealous need. He switched back to her clit, this time pressing a finger inside her damp well, spreading her. Her cunt was tight, the corrugated muscles rippling against his finger, massaging it in delicious waves.

"That's it," he all but purred as he lifted his head. She was breathing in short, sharp gasps. He plunged a second finger in, and she writhed against the invasion, moving her head back and forth on the pillow, her eyes closed. "Come for me, Nadia."

He went back down, nibbling on her, then closing his mouth on her clit and sucking hard, massaging the taut nubbin with his tongue.

Her scream was piercing, and he felt the flood of her release douse his fingers as his mouth kept working, drawing out the orgasm. She clenched like a clamp around his fingers, and he wanted nothing more than to bury himself in her hot, tight pussy. Still, the feeling of triumph, knowing that she was still experiencing the aftershocks of the orgasm he'd given her, knowing that every single shared moment made her more his. That knowledge was more intoxicating than thirty-year-old Scotch. He drank every drop of her.

Her flesh was still feverish when he slid up on top of her, his cock nuzzling between her thighs, blunt tip nudging at her wet entrance. "Nadia," he breathed. "Don't be frightened of me."

He paused at the brink of her cunt, frowning. He hadn't meant to say that.

She looked at him, her expression one of desperation and helplessness. Her hands were still under the pillow, still behind her head. He stared at her, feeling a sudden sense of unease.

Closing her eyes, she withdrew her hands, and linked them behind his neck. "Dominic," she murmured softly.

It was an act of submission. *"Nadia,"* he growled, kissing her fiercely. She met his kiss with just as much passion, her tongue reaching for his, tangling with his. She nipped at his lower lip.

His cock wouldn't be restrained anymore. He plunged into her still-wet passageway with one firm, deep thrust. She screamed against his mouth, one of pain and pleasure inextricably meshed together.

The feel of her tightness constricting against him was almost enough to push him over the edge. He held still, fighting for control. "Did I hurt you?" he muttered before he gave in completely to the mindless monster clawing to be released.

"Fuck me, Dominic," she said instead. "Make me forget."

His body strained to the breaking point, but his mind pressed forward with one last question. "Forget what?"

She wrapped her legs around his waist, her fingernails digging into his shoulders. "Forget everything," she responded, and to his shock, he felt her body *pulse* around him, gripping him in a ripple of muscles that danced and clasped around his cock like nothing he'd ever felt before.

He started moving, his hips arching and pumping into her, and she met him beat for beat. His hands held her hips tight as his cock slid in and out of her snug pussy. Her legs twined around his. She was climbing on him, trying to get closer. He got on his knees, lifting her hips off the bed, straining to get closer. She whimpered with encouragement as he shifted her, moving her ankle over his shoulder, giving him even deeper access to her. He plunged inside of her, his thumb seeking out and finding her clit as he pushed and strained, his cock rubbing the inside walls of her pussy with reckless, random, incredible strokes. He felt the wetness dripping against his balls, and he heard her cry out as another orgasm rippled through her. *"Yes!"* she screamed, gripping his headboard.

"Not . . . yet . . ." he growled at his own body, which was screaming for release. Instead, he surprised her by putting her leg back around his waist, then picking her up, holding her tight against his kneeling body. She constricted herself around his waist, meeting his kiss with an animalistic fury. The kiss was like napalm, scorching, all consuming. He felt her tongue twined with his as she impaled herself around his cock, her hips straining against his. He let out a roar as his orgasm tore through him, his cock jerking inside her as his cum spurt viciously from his body. She held him tight, her hips ramming against his as he came.

For a second, he almost blacked out. They tumbled to the bed, sweaty, still enmeshed in each other. His head was buried in the crook of her neck, each frantic, panting breath making him inhale more of her sweet scent.

God. She was incredible.

Concerned he might be crushing her, he rolled her on top of him, settling himself onto her pillow. He felt drained, completely wrung out . . . and unbelievably light. It was a strange feeling. He felt her heartbeat slowing and evening out with his. He caressed her ass, imagining giving it a light, playful swat.

Later, he thought. He had plenty of time. And that was an incredibly arousing thought—that he could take his time. That he'd be able to enjoy her for as long as he wanted.

Unconsciously, he stretched a hand behind his head, beneath his pillow . . . then yelped when his fingertips connected with something sharp.

He sat up, dumping Nadia off his cock unceremoniously. "What . . ." She protested, then stopped abruptly.

He threw the pillow off the bed, revealing the knife she'd

been hiding underneath it. He picked it up, showing it to her.

"Have an explanation for this?"

I shouldn't be here.

"He'll see you now," an efficient-looking young woman said, standing in the foyer of the modern-looking mansion. It was much larger than her house. She frowned. Rather, it was much larger than Henry's house—he would no doubt protest calling it "her" house—and this mansion was obviously much more luxurious.

It belonged to Phillipe Wright, owner of a series of high-class restaurants and clubs, a multimillionaire in his own right and heir to a large, old-money European family fortune. He was rich, rumored to be eccentric, and known to be powerful in both legitimate circles and more illicit company.

Her palms sweated. She tried not to rub them accidentally on the deep crimson of her raw silk business suit. Instead, she gripped the handle of her Hermès bag more tightly, and fought to look controlled. She followed the redheaded woman down a hallway, to what was obviously an office. Light wood paneling, mahogany furniture, discreet and tasteful black and white photos on the walls . . . and a huge desk that he was sitting behind, like some banker waiting to review her loan application, or a CEO about to conduct an interview.

He knew this wasn't a social call. And he wanted her to know where she stood.

"Jelena Granville," he said, his tone cultured, with the slightest hint of an accent. He was in his late forties, good-looking in a rugged sort of way—Robert Redford when he'd started to lose his pretty-boy looks. His eyes were shrewd, twinkling with almost merriment. "When I gave you my home address, I thought that you said you'd never stoop to contacting me, so this is a pleasant surprise."

Her cheeks flared with heat. The one time she'd met him had been at a party Henry had somehow wrangled an invitation to. Henry was trying too hard to make connections, to network—to get a leg up in the social circle. Everyone there had known it, and Jelena had been horribly embarrassed. When Phillipe had shown an interest in her, Henry had misunderstood, thinking that she could somehow make him more popular with the eccentric millionaire. He'd encouraged her to have a private drink with the man.

"You're beautiful," Phillipe had said, once they were alone, giving her an intense visual perusal. "Why waste time with him?"

Him being her husband.

She'd been younger then, and while she'd felt flattered, she'd also felt insulted. "He is my husband," she'd informed Phillipe, in frosty tones.

"Of course he is." Phillipe's smile had been like cream in rich coffee, rich and seductive. "Come upstairs for a moment. Have sex with me."

She'd goggled, purely shocked.

"Aren't you sweet," he'd said, when she spluttered out a refusal, and she hadn't thought he'd meant it as a compliment. Then he'd handed her a card with his address written on the back. "If you get tired of your keeper, call me. When you're not feeling quite so sweet."

He'd walked away from her. She'd never told Henry.

She'd never thrown away the card, either.

She sat in one of the leather seats opposite Phillipe, her purse in her lap. "I need your help," she said, her voice quavering slightly. She had not figured out a more graceful way to couch the request, so she simply plunged forward. "My sister has been taken hostage."

His eyes widened. "I'm sorry?"

"She's been taken by a man named Dominic Luder," she said, and noticed the way his face went from shocked to carefully blank. "I think you know him. You know everyone," she pressed. "I know that you can help me. Please, please help me!"

He still stared at her, the slight cast in his otherwise placid face suggesting distaste. "That's why you called, set up an appointment to see me? You want my *help*?"

"Yes," she said, her voice breaking. Tears filled her eyes.

He sighed deeply. Then he got up, walked around the desk, and leaned on the surface of it as he looked at her.

"Do I look like a white knight to you?"

"I don't know what you mean," she breathed. "I just . . . I didn't know who else to turn to."

"I'm powerful, I know everything, so you decided to ask me for a favor," he said, and his expression looked bored.

Jelena looked into her lap to see her hands mangling the strap of her purse. She bit her lip and looked back at him.

"What were you planning to offer, in exchange for this favor?"

"Anything," she said. "Anything you wanted."

He quirked one aristocratic eyebrow.

She swallowed against the lump in her throat. This, she had on some level expected.

She lowered her eyes to the floor, then her hands went to the buttons on her blouse. She unbuttoned them slowly, starting at her neckline and moving lower.

She felt his broad hands closing over hers, stopping her.

"I see," he said, with a hint of a chuckle. Obviously, he could—the lace of her bra and still-bountiful breasts were clearly evident. Her heart raced, and she looked up.

There was a hint of a smile. No, the hint of a *smirk*, etched in his handsome, weathered face.

"So brave," he murmured. "So willing."

She tensed. His words did not sound complimentary.

"I've done some research on you, Jelena," he said, releasing her hands as his knuckles barely brushed over the slopes of her breasts. Involuntarily, her nipples tightened. "Your marriage was an arrangement, wasn't it? Your family is from Russia?"

"Yes." She swallowed. "Yes, to both."

"You're absolutely stunning. He's lucky to have gotten you for such a low price," Phillipe said, his voice briskly businesslike, and she jolted slightly. "But you lack a certain . . . spirit, shall we say."

Despair warred with anger. "Are you going to help me," she said, in a quiet voice, "or just insult me?"

He cupped her cheek with his hand, his thumb framing her jaw and chin. "You have the face of an angel," he whispered.

She had never slept with anyone but her husband, her virginity being yet another bargaining chip in her marriage. But she felt inexorably drawn to this man . . . his strength, his aura of incredible power.

He leaned close, whispering in her ear like a lover.

"Unfortunately," he murmured, "I'm not interested in angels."

She pulled away from the warmth of his touch, getting to her feet. "What is this to you? Some game?" she snarled. "What do you want from me?"

"At the moment, nothing," he said, and that amusement was in his voice again, derisive. Corrosive. "Beauty is all well and good, but power . . . now, that is truly alluring. Something I've never been able to turn away from."

She crossed her arms in front of her open blouse. "If I had power," she said slowly, "you would help me."

He made a little gesture. "Perhaps."

She started to button up again, her fingers shaking slightly from both adrenaline and nerves.

If I had power, I wouldn't need you.

"And how do you define power, exactly?" she finally asked. "What would it take to prove that I have it?"

Now his smile was catlike. "There aren't any hard and fast rules to power. You know it when you see it." He gestured around. "Take me, for example. You knew I was powerful."

"You're rich," she said, trying not to let fury color her voice too much. "Well connected."

He shrugged. "That's part of it."

"I'm rich, too."

"No," he corrected. "Your husband is rich. Once he's gone, how rich will you be?"

She felt a wave of ice wash over her. *Isn't that what you were just thinking about?*

He nodded, seeing that his point was made. "Power is more than money, Jelena. It's will. Determination." His eyes glittered like diamonds, bright and cold. "A willingness to do what others will not."

She gritted her teeth. She had lived her life doing whatever was required of her. Did he really think she was so weak that she would simply cry when asked to do something unpleasant?

"Maybe it's time to stop playing the good girl, Jelena. Time to take control of your own fate."

She closed her eyes. It was like he was reading her mind. She didn't like it, but felt strangely compelled by it as well.

He walked behind her, and whispered at her again. "The marriage is trapping you. Being a good girl has done you no good at all. Perhaps it's time to break some rules to get what you want."

She shivered. She couldn't help it. She leaned back against him, felt his body, hard as granite behind her. He stroked her arms.

Then he nudged her away from him. "I've got another appointment," he murmured. "But please, feel free to get in contact with me if you feel your situation has, ah, changed."

She blinked. Just like that, she'd been dismissed.

She picked up her purse, feeling bereft—no. Horrified.

She stepped out of the office, her heels clicking on the parquet floors.

The red-haired assistant was leading a different woman down the hallway. A tall, stunning woman, with jet black hair. She looked predatory, and the closer Jelena looked, the more unnatural the beauty appeared.

The woman glanced over at Jelena, sending a sneering appraisal with a curl of her plump lips. "What are you looking at?" she said sharply.

Ordinarily, Jelena would have apologized for rudeness. Now she felt anger leap to the fore. She glared at the woman.

The woman took a step away from her, then quickly followed the assistant.

Maybe that was it, Jelena thought as she got back in her car. She had gone to the devil, expecting him to be merciful, to help her in her time of need. Instead, she had no one to rely on but herself.

Well, she was tired of waiting to be saved. She was tired of being a pawn, and watching her sisters get played on the same chessboard she stood on. *It is time to be queened,* she thought. Have the power to do whatever she wanted.

For that, you're going to need money.

Her husband had money. He'd cut her off without a cent, given the chance.

She started the engine, her mind starting to work furiously.

The answer: get money before he gets the chance.

Chapter Four

"Nadia. Come with me."

She nodded at Dominic's cold words, following him naked into the hallway. He looked like the Angel of Death. No, not an angel. An angel would be beautiful. He looked powerful, and fearsome, and unforgiving. His blue eyes burned incandescently every time he looked at her.

He was going to punish her. She didn't know how, and the dreadful anticipation carved into her, leaving her raw.

"What were you going to do with this, Nadia?" he had said, his voice taunting yet furious. "Planning to kill me with a paring knife?"

She hadn't responded. She hadn't needed to.

Why didn't you try killing him when you had the chance?

Not that it would have worked, she thought as she padded

silently after Dominic. He would have easily been able to disarm her. But when he was having sex with her, he wouldn't have suspected it. She could have gone for his throat, for his eye. She could have done *something* to kill him. Done something to eliminate the threat that was looming over her family.

She felt tears edge from the corners of her eyes, and wiped them away hastily.

You didn't think about it when he was fucking you, did you? You couldn't think of anything else.

She bit her lip, hard, the pain keeping her emotions at bay. *You let him do this to you. You failed them all.*

Dominic had left with the knife, anger evident in every inch of his carved body. "I can't just leave this unpunished, Nadia," he said, and then he'd shut the door, locking it. She hadn't slept, waiting for morning and his promise.

Would he hurt her? Would he hurt them? God, what had she done?

He led her to the large, tile-floored foyer. Was he going to throw her out, naked, to find her way in the desert? Where were they anyway? She felt her palms begin to sweat.

He turned to her. "The floor here is filthy," he drawled, his eyes still trained on her like a hawk. She glanced down. The floor was anything but—she doubted there was a speck of dirt anywhere in the house. She waited.

He pulled out a bucket filled with clear water, and a washcloth, the size that one washed her face with. She glanced at him.

"My punishment is to clean your floor?"

"Do you have a problem with that?"

"No." If anything, she felt relieved. Manual labor was easy. It was . . .

"You're not quite finished yet," he said softly.

She paused in reaching for the washcloth, looking at him speculatively.

He was handing her a pair of stiletto heels. She stared at them in bewilderment. "You want me to wash the floor in these?"

"Among other things."

She shrugged. She'd be on her knees most of the time anyway, she reasoned as she slipped on the imposing looking shoes. Besides, it would obviously give him some prurient satisfaction, and anything that . . .

"You're not through yet," he interrupted her train of thought. "I've got one more piece of equipment for you."

Her eyes widened as she stared at the contraption he held in front of her. "What is *that*?"

"You put a leg in each strap . . ." he explained, then smiled, slowly, harshly. "Here. I'll just put it on you."

She swallowed hard. Between the straps was a pink plastic dildo with some kind of attachment on it, like a little Y near the base. The device was not quite as large as Dominic, but still large enough to give her pause. He expected her to wear that thing—no, to *take* that thing—as she knelt down in the torturously sexy high heels, scrubbing his floor.

This was the real punishment. And she got the sense it was just the beginning.

He knelt in front of her, guiding her hands to his shoulders, lifting her feet as he slipped the straps over first one foot, then the other. He eased the toy up between her thighs, and she felt the cool plastic graze her sensitive flesh. She was still a little tender from her bout of lovemaking with . . .

Sex, she corrected herself. *Not lovemaking*. She was still tender from *fucking* Dominic.

"Hmmm. Might need a little help here," he muttered, as if he were a mechanic. Then, without warning, he started rubbing her pussy, spreading the lips of her labia and massaging her clit with ruthless intensity.

She gasped, clutching at his shoulders as he circled her slowly, carefully, with the innate skill that made her lose her mind. How did he manage that? Was it with all women—or was she simply too susceptible to his touch?

"That's better," he announced, then urged her thighs to spread wider. He maneuvered the dildo against her, pressing in slowly, letting it glide deep inside her. She felt the attachment, nestled up against her clit. He spread her further, and she felt either side of the Y close snugly against her clit. When it was all adjusted to his satisfaction, he stood up.

"There," he said. "You might want to start by the door and work your way toward the living room."

She could see the deep blush that stained her skin. Awkwardly, she knelt down on all fours, unable to keep her legs clamped together because of the device. She could feel his hot gaze sliding over her as she began to scrub, the warm cloth moving in slow circles against the cold stone tiles.

She did a few squares of tile, then reached for the bucket, glancing over her shoulder. He was staring at her, as she expected. However, he was holding something. She paused, trying to figure out what it was. It looked like a remote, she realized. He smiled, then hit a button.

Suddenly, the attachment clamped on her clit started to flutter, slowly at first, then vibrating more enthusiastically. She felt it like a sensual slap. "Oh!" she cried, dropping the cloth into the bucket with a splash.

"Don't forget near the baseboards," he said, in a bored tone of voice, even as the rhythm of the vibrator increased.

She didn't answer, picking up the cloth instead. She moved slowly, carefully, trying to ignore the delicious, dizzying pressure of the vibrator as it hummed against her. Her body felt like it was on fire, every nerve ending hyper-aware. She bit her lip, trying not to moan as the incredible feelings licked over her.

"Hmm." He walked toward her, nudging her hand. "Missed a spot."

She wiped at where he'd gestured. As she stretched, he pushed another button.

Suddenly, the dildo inside her was moving, first clockwise, then counterclockwise, shifting and twisting as it filled her. She let out a low cry of pleasure, then shut her eyes tight, cleaning blindly.

He moved to stand in front of her. He was wearing slacks and expensive Italian shoes, and all she wanted to do was jump up and attack him. Not to kill him . . . no. To force him to finish the sexual torture he was inflicting on her.

Have you no loyalty? Don't you know what this man is?

She stared at the floor as if her life depended on it.

"How does it feel, knowing I can do this to you whenever I want?" she heard him ask. "Knowing that whatever I ask you to do, you have to do . . . or you'll pay the consequences?"

She didn't answer. The cloth moved across the floor slowly, erasing spots that did not exist.

"Your body is mine," he repeated. "I can take you whenever and however I want."

Right, left. The cloth went back in the bucket.

He flicked another switch, and everything increased . . . the dildo sped up, the vibrator thrummed against her clit mercilessly. She gasped, her eyes going half-lidded.

He shut it off. "I can also withhold things from you."

No! she wanted to cry out. She gripped the washcloth like a vise, her body shrieking in unfulfilled torment.

He got in front of her, unzipping his pants. His cock sprung free. "I can tell you to do things to me."

She stared at his enormous cock, thrusting in front of her. Then she looked at him.

"Taste me," he instructed.

He wanted to punish her. Did he not know that she was so turned on, that *he turned her on so much*, that even this was more pleasure than punishment?

She didn't hesitate, her body already going for him, her mouth latching on to the tip of his cock and circling it, her tongue tracing around the rim of its bulbous head, tickling the fissure at the tip. His moan of pleasure was tinged with surprise. He fisted his hands against his sides, inadvertently flicking the switch again. She gasped against his hot, hard flesh as the dildo and vibrator started up again, causing a tornado of sexual sensation to crash through her.

She started to move, taking him in deep enough to gag. Letting go of the washcloth, she gripped his penis in both hands, stroking him eagerly, hungrily. Her hands slid up and down his shaft. One reached down to cup his balls, exploring them, then tickling the delicate flesh just behind them. He groaned loudly, leaning back, his hips arching toward her. He increased the pressure of her toy.

She pulled away from him for a second, gasping as the pressure of her building orgasm singed her. She was close . . . so close . . .

"Don't stop," he ordered, guiding her head back to his swollen erection. She started working on him, devouring him, savoring every masculine taste of him. He shifted his hips, nudging deeper against her mouth, and she nibbled at him, mindless with her own pleasure but still careful enough to only let the edges of her teeth graze his flesh. Groaning, he lost his balance, falling against the wall. She gripped him, not letting go, increasing her suction softly as she moved faster against his shaft, her tongue dancing and flicking over his feverish skin.

He increased the setting to the highest level. She growled against his cock, the vibrato of her voice matching the hum of the toy currently buzzing its way against her core. She made hot, animal-like noises against him. Her tongue seduced his cock as the toy was seducing her. She was breathing hard, almost insane with the intensity of her desire.

Finally, she was pushed over the edge. The dildo pressed against just the right spot, and her clit was shivering with sensation, and the orgasm shot through her, starting at her cunt and seeping out toward her every extremity. She pulled away, screaming, gasping with ecstasy. Her hands gripped his cock, urging the hard flesh, rubbing it frantically.

"*Nadia,*" he yelled, eyes closed, head back. The cum spurted out of him, across her chest, down her breasts. She glistened with the iridescent liquid. She held him as he quivered, bathed in the hot drops, shuddering and panting with the aftershocks of her own climax.

He leaned back, his breathing labored, his cock still gleaming from her mouth.

She held him, resting her forehead against his strong upper thigh. Softly, so softly that he couldn't possibly have noticed, she pressed a tiny kiss against him.

The device stopped with a snap. Wordlessly, he lifted her up, then removed it from her body. He held it in his hands, looking at her.

"I own you," he said, in a low, solemn voice.

She looked away. He nudged her face until her eyes met his, gleaming like a wizard's stare.

"I own you," he repeated, "because you can't help yourself. Because I can do things to your body that you can't even imagine."

He kissed her, hard, and she felt her whole body shake with the pleasure of it. It ended as quickly as it began.

"Don't try a stunt like that again," he whispered, his breath hot against her ear, her neck. "Stronger people than you have been trying to kill me for years, and they haven't succeeded yet. Your best bet for survival is to make sure I'm satisfied, Nadia. That's what you should be focusing your energy on."

With that, he walked away. She swore the son of a bitch was whistling under his breath.

She kicked the bucket across the floor, swearing in Russian.

I own you because you can't help yourself.

"Bastard!" she growled from between clenched teeth. Then she looked, saw the sodden mess she'd made.

"You'll be cleaning that up, Nadia." His voice floated ghostly from the far end of the hall.

She wanted to scream. Now, she *really* regretted not killing him.

She headed for the kitchen, grumbling, searching for a mop to clean up the foyer. Her mind whirred.

He was right: no one had ever made her feel the way he did. Her body still shivered with sensual aftershocks. If it were any other situation, she'd gladly give herself over to the pleasure he seemed able to coax from her with no effort whatsoever. It scared her, to think about how easily she'd give herself over to his control.

But he was messing with her family, the one thing she had dedicated her life and well-being to protecting. Now, he thought to make her feel inferior? To taunt her with the threat that, if she didn't keep him "satisfied," he would exact a crueler punishment?

Fuck that.

Her eyes narrowed. Oh, she'd make sure he was satisfied. She might not have had a lot of experience with the pleasures of seduction, but she was a damned fast learner. Before she was done, he'd be just as snared as she was.

She smiled coldly.

And then, I'll destroy him.

"Mrs. Granville. So nice to see you," Henry's accountant, Robert, said with a small, puzzled smile. "And, er, unexpected."

Jelena smiled at him, feeling a little at loose ends herself.

How am I supposed to pull this off?

"Is there anything the matter?" Robert prompted, his sandy blond hair falling in front of his glasses, making him look young and almost vulnerable. "I mean . . . with your account? Did you have any problems with your allow—" He stopped himself, coughing on the word. "I mean . . . with your . . . er, deposit?"

Allowance. A grown woman, receiving an allowance. Good grief, is this what she'd come to?

She shook her head. "No, Robert. I received my allowance"—irony tinged her words—"just as I have every month for the six years."

"Good." Now he looked thoroughly baffled. "So, um, how can I help you?"

"That is the question," she said, simply, sitting in the chair across from his desk. "How can you help me?"

"I'm a-afraid I don't understand," he stammered, as she stared at him.

She needed his help. But he was Henry's accountant,

wasn't he? What in the world would convince him to help her? She had no leverage. She had nothing. She . . .

She was staring at his face, deep in her own thoughts, when she noticed that he was avoiding staring at her. When he did look at her, it was a quick, almost hungry look. A searching look.

She licked her lips, without thinking.

He stared involuntarily, and she watched his Adam's apple bob as he swallowed hard. He fidgeted with his tie. Then, it seemed, he realized he was staring, and he quickly shuffled papers on his desk. "I . . . I don't understand," he repeated.

"I need money," she said softly. "I need help. Your help."

And she finally thought she saw where she might get some leverage.

She stood, slowly, uncertainly. She hadn't tried to seduce Phillip—she had begged, she had offered, but she hadn't seduced. No wonder he had said she was a martyr, a victim.

She'd been told she was beautiful, but it was something that was simply there—like having blond hair or hazel eyes. It was a fact. Now, as she approached the young man and saw his color go hectic, a slight flush covering his throat and cheeks, she realized that being beautiful was more than a simple description.

Beauty was a tool. She'd used it passively, the coin to purchase safety, security.

She needed to use it as a weapon.

She sat at the edge of the desk, close to him, at the same time wondering if she were being too obvious and campy.

She'd hate to be coming across as some bad parody of *The Graduate*.

"Henry is cheating on me," she said, putting in words what she'd only suspected. "Sometime in the future, probably soon, he will divorce me and replace me. He will leave me penniless if he can."

Robert made a little noise of embarrassed protest. She waved it away, her throat constricting with emotion.

"My sister is in trouble," she whispered. She should be seducing him, not pleading, right? But she couldn't help it. He seemed so sincere, staring at her. "I need your help, Robert. Is there anything you can do to help me?"

He stood up, staring into her eyes. Then he took a step away from her.

She watched as he headed for the door, despair gnawing at her. Would he kick her out, then? What else could she do?

But instead of turning the door handle, he locked it. Then he looked back at her, with a helpless, overwhelming hunger that made her smile, a touch wickedly. When was the last time anyone had looked at her like that?

Never. Henry's desire was completely self-centered, a performance rather than a gift.

She felt her own hunger stoked by Robert's evident admiration. She felt a warm glow of confidence start to burn in her chest.

"Maybe there's something I could do to help," he muttered, walking back to his desk . . . back to *her*. He stood next to her, a flush of pink across his cheeks, but his eyes were determined. "Your husband has a lot of different accounts.

He never pays attention, just tells me to 'handle everything' and not bother him with the details." The resentment in his voice told her just how her husband had "handled" working with his accountant. Henry always wanted someone to give orders to. Someone he expected obedience from.

Oh, yes, Robert would help her. She felt a surge of something deliciously unfamiliar at the thought. *Passion?*

No. *Power.* So this was what Phillipe was talking about.

"If some of his money was to get temporarily misplaced," Robert murmured, "he wouldn't notice. Especially if it weren't in the monthly report that he doesn't miss anyway. As long as he had his spending money . . ." Robert cleared his throat, then looked at her, a small, mischievous smile on his face.

"Thank you, Robert," her voice purred, approvingly. Would it be that easy, then? She wanted to kiss him with gratitude.

"But it's putting my job on the line," he interrupted. "I'm taking a lot of risk here. Once he found out—and he would— then my reputation would be ruined. He's one of my biggest clients, and I've got a small firm here. I couldn't just . . ."

She frowned, irritated. Was he backing out, then? "What are you saying, Robert?"

He sighed, looked away—then looked back at her. "I would need, er, a *really* good reason to do this," he said.

She stared at him, not comprehending.

He seemed to steel himself, taking a deep breath. Then he reached out, fondling her breast lightly, tentatively. His palm froze over her nipple, and he stared at her, questioning.

She closed her eyes, not wanting to show triumph. It was too easy, really.

"Do you want me, then, Robert?" she found herself saying softly. "Do you want something specific, in exchange for helping a woman in distress?"

His eyes widened, and she felt his hand tremble against her. Then, without a word, he moved forward, kissing her with a hard fierceness she would not have expected from such a wiry, prepossessing-looking young man.

His mouth was firm on hers, his tongue teasing her lips, his hand increasing its pressure on her breast as he nudged her back further onto his desk. The door was locked. He wasn't expecting anyone to interrupt.

It would be here, then.

She parted her legs, and he stepped easily between them. He reached down, fingers digging into her hip as he tugged her against him. She felt his erection, a sizable hardness, surprising her. And, even more surprising, her body went wet at the sensation.

In the past six years, every episode of sex with Henry had felt orchestrated—when he wanted, how he wanted. She was barely a participant. This was different. More urgent. More real. She wasn't sure how else to describe it. It was simply *more*.

She kissed back, hard, and heard him growl against her lips as her hands went up to remove his tie, undo the buttons of his shirt until she could press her palms against the hot skin of his chest. He did the same, undoing the buttons on her blouse, taking it off, leaving her in just her skirt. She shifted her weight, wriggling, shoving her skirt up her waist and tearing off the panties that got in the way.

"Jelena," he breathed against her hair as he tore off his shirt and coat, undoing his pants and letting them drop to the floor. He was hard, jutting out against her. She stared. She hadn't seen anyone's penis but Henry's in . . . well, ever. She studied it, cupping it in her palm, circling it with her fingers. He groaned, leaning against her. It felt like hot velvet. A bead glistened at the fissure at the tip.

She lifted the bead to her lips with a fingertip, then tasted it with her tongue.

He took off her skirt, leaving her naked on top of his desk as he kicked off his shoes and the rest of his clothes. "God, I've wanted you," he breathed, kissing her again, his hands stroking her chest, her waist. She could feel the hot length of his cock against her thigh.

"Condom," she breathed, not so far gone that she wasn't thinking of that.

He chuckled, somewhat embarrassed. Then he opened a desk drawer, producing a foil package. He tore it open with his teeth, then rolled the membrane on.

She expected him to simply go at it: stick it in, get it over with. Instead, he reached down, between her thighs, his fingers parting the darker blond curls over her sex. His touch was gentle but probing. He felt the folds of her, feeling the beginning dampness. He kissed her, distracting her as his fingers slowly plunged deeper, brushing past her sensitive clit, wakening her. Arousing her. She melted against him, her legs starting to circle his, drawing his cock closer to her increasingly wet slot. He laughed against her lips, his free hand cupping one breast and kneading it, gently, thoroughly.

She started to breathe harder, her body jolting at the sensation. She had expected enduring the sex, as a price for the cash . . . as a price for her sister's freedom and safety. She had not expected to enjoy it. She certainly hadn't expected to enjoy it as much as she currently was. Her hips bucked against his hand as his fingers probed deeper, rubbing against her clit, pushing against her inside.

"More," she urged, as her body got into the sway of it. Her legs wrapped around his waist, drawing him inexorably closer. "Please."

"You like this?" he teased.

To her surprise, he tugged her, pulling her off the desk. She stood flat on her bare feet. He nudged her around, leaning her over the desk.

Her body felt cold without his hand delving inside her. *This,* she thought, *would be less enjoyable.*

But she was wrong, again. He entered her slowly, but one hand still snaked around her, searching out and finding her clit as he carefully entered her, inch by inch. As he filled her, her body still felt a delicious stirring. He moaned when he finally buried himself to the hilt, his hips brushing the back of her buttocks. Her breasts were pressed against the cold granite of his desktop, her waist balanced along the edge, blocked only by his wrist as he continued to manipulate her clit. He withdrew almost the whole way, then pressed back in, slowly. She sighed when he filled her, and whimpered, ever so slightly, when he retreated.

His pace was relentlessly patient. He stroked inside her calmly, even as her blood began to race and her body began to heat, wanting more than he was giving her. Her breathing went ragged. She backed up against him as he pumped behind her, constantly resisting the enticing wriggle of her ass as she muttered for him to push more, harder, fill her . . .

He stopped, only the tip inside her. "Do you like this?" he said, and she could tell he was taunting her . . . drawing it out.

She slammed back, forcing him inside her with a swift plunge that was almost painful, and they both groaned in response. "I want to feel your cock ramming inside me," she ordered in a rough purr. "I want you to make me come."

He seemed shocked by the order. Aroused by it.

She'd succeeded in breaking his control. Suddenly, he was plunging into her, grabbing her waist and pulling her against his cock. She breathed hard, trying to catch up as he slammed home, angling with her, forcing her against the desk. She was on the elusive edge, but there was something that wasn't working. Something that wasn't right. She wanted to tell him to stop, to wait, but it was a bit too late.

She could feel it when he came. He let out a low, surprised grunt, and then shuddered against her uncontrollably, collapsing on top her of her, crushing her against his desk.

She frowned. That was exciting.

And, well, a bit disappointing.

He withdrew finally, and when she turned, he was all business, getting dressed. She got dressed, too.

"I can get you all the money you need," he promised, his voice fervent.

"Thank you."

He suddenly looked young and hopeful. "When can I see you again?"

"Soon," she said gently. She kissed him, and he seemed to sway against her. She nudged him away.

When she got back to her car, she flipped open her cell phone, dialing Phillipe's number.

"Jelena," he greeted her, his cultured voice smooth as satin. "I wasn't expecting to hear from you so . . ."

"I've started to get the money," she said. "One hundred thousand. I can get more." She gritted her teeth. "I intend to get more."

He seemed startled. "What does that have to do with me?"

"I don't have time—" She bit off the sentence. He didn't care about her timelines—didn't care about Nadia's life. She took a deep breath. "You're interested in women with power. I'm interested in learning about it. I wanted to know if you might also be interested in giving me some lessons."

He paused, and she could sense he was intrigued. Men and their egos. He didn't want to help her, but he couldn't resist being seen as a master.

"All right," he said. "Come to my house tonight. And I'll teach you a few things."

She hung up. She'd learn fast. She'd save Nadia.

But first, she thought, she was going to take some steps. She had money now.

She dialed another number, and started to set her trap.

Chapter Five

"You missed a spot."

Nadia glanced over at him, a smile already on her lips. She looked polite, inquisitive. Like an employee at a hotel, eager and willing to somehow make sure his experience was exemplary.

He grinned. She didn't fool him for a moment. She was many things, but subservient never made the list.

"Where?" she finally asked, her voice several shades of sweetness. As if nothing on earth would please her more than to clean up after him.

He nodded over to the bookcase. She moved with careful precision, using the feather duster in one hand to brush away the imagined dirt. It was a painfully slow process, given the fact that she had a spacer bar over her shoulders, with both wrists attached at either end with leather restraints. The bar latched to a collar rigged around her throat.

It was a joke, sort of. He still hadn't quite forgiven her for the paring knife incident. Granted, there was absolutely no way she would have been able to kill him with the paltry little weapon. Still, it was the thought behind it.

There was still a standing, open hit out on him, had been for the past three years. He'd be damned if he got capped in his sleep by a pretty little brunette amateur because he'd gotten careless and let his dick do his thinking.

She dropped the feather duster. She sighed softly, then got down on her knees, carefully maneuvering to awkwardly pick it back up. The position—kneeling, naked, with the black spacer bar spreading her arms—was unbelievably arousing.

That hadn't exactly been the point, either, but he certainly wasn't complaining about the results.

When she got back up, he noticed another nice side benefit of the bar. It forced her to arch her back slightly, her breasts jutting forward in delectable presentation. She smiled slowly, a smile full of promise, and she looked down, hiding her eyes with her thick fringe of lashes. God, she was beautiful.

He went hard in a rush. He was a walking erection these days, he thought ruefully.

That, also, hadn't been part of the plan.

"Is there anything else I can do for you?" she drawled, her voice low and husky and inviting. She shot him a look that was calculatedly coy.

What are you up to?

"I don't know," he drawled. "I guess that's all for today."

He forced himself to sound bored, even though a careful look would obviously show the stiffness straining against his fly. He walked up to her, quickly removing the wrist restraints and unlatching the bar from her collar. He left the collar on, though. It seemed to go so nicely with the black patent leather heels she wore.

And of course you'd notice that, you idiot.

He was about to send her away, when she walked a little too close, her hip brushing against him. His hand shot out involuntarily, catching her wrist. It was barely a grip, but she stopped immediately.

"Yes?" she breathed.

He leaned down, close to her face. "You're planning something," he murmured, smelling the sweet perfume that was obviously pure Nadia. "You're plotting."

"Am I?" Her look of innocence was still belied by the piercing intelligence in her eyes.

"I don't underestimate people," he said, and found himself stroking her arm. Her skin was so unbelievably soft. He circled her shoulder with his thumb. "Trust me, I'll never underestimate you."

He was looking at her face when he said it, and something about that statement made her features soften, just for a flash. She cleared her throat. "I'm just a silly woman," she demurred, and he could sense the drop of bitterness her contradiction contained.

He shook his head. "You're brave enough to face me," he pointed out.

"Maybe just foolish."

"That, too," he agreed, grinning when her eyes snapped to his, glinting with irritation. "But strong. And loyal."

What would it be like, to have her loyalty?

She shrugged, but he held her chin. He looked into her eyes, and she didn't try to turn away. "Beautiful, too," he breathed against her throat.

He hadn't meant to say, or do, any of that. He released her, taking a careful step back. She was intoxicating—distracting. He needed to get some space.

But as he started to turn away, he noticed something. Her dusky rose nipples were hard, excited. If he looked carefully enough, he could see the slight glistening of wetness between her thighs.

She was wet. *For him.*

He didn't speak. He couldn't think. He simply stripped off his shirt, shucked off his pants, and reached for her, naked as she was.

He waited. She paused for only a moment before stepping into his embrace, pressing her breasts against his chest as she tilted her head up.

He kissed her harshly, the taste of her drugging him as his hands roamed over the soft skin of her stomach, the gentle curve of her hips as they flowed into her torso. He reached up to feel the crushed silk of her hair beneath his fingertips, weaving his hand in her locks to pull her closer, making the kiss deeper. She didn't shy away. Instead, he shuddered as she molded herself to his body, his cock nestled against the planes of her stomach. She was smooth, hot skin and need. Her hands slid up his chest, reaching up to his shoulders, gently scoring the skin with her rounded nails. He growled, wanting to devour her. Forcing himself to slow down, to savor every sensation.

He'd had beautiful women before, but not like this. Then, it had always been about his prowess: the subtle feeling of triumph, followed by the not-so-subtle feeling of the letdown as he inevitably left. Those women had looked at him as a sort of prize, or some wild beast they could capture and tame. He'd had no problems using them and leaving.

Then, Alexis . . . and the ultimate payback for his capriciousness. He winced, pulling away from Nadia as the memory jolted him out of the moment.

Nadia made an irritated sound of protest, pulling him back against her. Was she acting? He wondered at her hunger, at her sheer sensual honesty—and at the fire he'd seen in her eyes. He admired her for her courage, even as he resented her nobility. At first, he'd taken pleasure in trying to break her.

Now, he was simply taking pleasure.

She hooked one leg over his pelvis, trying to angle herself up. He felt her damp curls pulling against his thigh, and any sense of recrimination or caution flew out the window. The animal in him was unleashed—it had to be fed.

The floor was hard, but he didn't care. He stretched out on his clothes, tugging her on top of him. She parted her legs easily, straddling him, impaling herself on his rock-hard length. She lowered herself slowly, by inches. He growled in response to the pleasure coursing through him.

"Dominic," she breathed, raising herself on her knees, then lowering herself.

The feel of her wet heat stroking over his cock like a tight mouth was maddeningly sweet, intensely wonderful. His hips tensed and flexed. He reached up, stroking his palms over her hips, her waist, until he cupped her breasts, kneading them gently, tweaking the nipples. She trembled, and the sensation of her body shimmying against his was almost enough to make him come. He clamped down, forcing himself to focus.

She covered his hands with her own, making his actions a little rougher, a little harder, and he shivered, then frowned. She slammed down harder on his cock, driving him deeper into her, and he groaned again in the face of unbelievable pleasure. The little minx was driving him mad.

Letting out a little sound of impatience, she grabbed one of his hands again, then deliberately smacked the palm against her ass.

His eyes flew open, and he stared at her. "What do you think you're doing?"

She looked stubborn . . . insistent. She arched her back, and he could feel his cock stroke against the lining of her pussy wall. She pulled his hand back again.

"Don't . . ." But it was too late. She slapped his hand against her ass again, hard enough to make his palm tingle with warmth. She moaned softly.

Was she . . . no. She couldn't be enjoying it.

Could she?

He tamped down on the wild delight that the thought sent through his body. She was smart. He'd been "punishing" her, using fetish accoutrements. She was upping the ante:

trying to show him that punishing her wouldn't work if the subject enjoyed every second of her degradation.

Damn, she's brilliant.

But he'd been playing games longer than she—and he wasn't about to be defeated.

He slapped her ass, lightly, just enough to hold a slight sting. He grinned as he did it, looking at her in challenge.

She didn't notice. Her eyes were closed, and she shivered, her motions against his cock growing quicker, jerkier. Her breasts still jutted out at him. He leaned up, taking one of the nipples in his mouth, suckling softly, circling the hard little rock of her nipple with his tongue. Then he spanked her again, a short, sharp stroke, as he caressed her nipple.

Now she let go with a full throated moan of pleasure as her pussy clenched around his. He felt the flood of wetness trickling down his cock, and he shook.

She came. She came from the dueling sensations of pleasure and pain. She was still shaking, her body clenching against him in waves, her eyes closed, her face drenched in pleasure.

He sat up, and she wrapped her legs around his waist. His cock was buried in her so deep he couldn't stand it. He wove his fingers into her hair, tugging gently, then more firmly. She gasped, exposing her throat. He pulled her tight against him, rocking her cunt over him as he sucked hard at her neck. She wriggled as if struggling, and he slowed his pressure, wondering if he'd gone too far.

"*More,*" she yelled, her hips gyrating wildly against him.

He sucked hard, his hips pumping furiously against her.

She clawed at his shoulders, screaming his name as her nipples dragged against his chest. She bucked against him, and she shrieked in pleasure as the next orgasm overwhelmed her. It was enough to shove him over the edge, into oblivion. He almost bit her as his climax shot through him, and he crushed her tight against his chest, groaning loudly against her skin as his hips jerked hard against hers with his release.

In the aftermath, they sat like that, on the hard floor of the solarium, entwined around each other, his cock buried deep inside her. Her head collapsed against his shoulder, and he held her tightly, as if he never wanted to let her go. He started kissing her shoulders, her throat, the valley between her breasts. He started kissing her mouth, slowly. He didn't want the sensation to end.

What the hell are you doing?

He stopped abruptly. It had felt so good—so amazing.

"Son of a bitch," he muttered to himself.

She opened her eyes slowly, her entire expression sleepy. "What?" she asked.

"Damn it. You're a fucking Oscar winner, aren't you?" He felt anger swirl through him—not at her, but at his own stupidity.

For a second there, he'd really wanted to believe it. Wanted to buy that she wanted him. That this was a different situation.

"You really thought you could manipulate me," he said, and his words grew sharper. "You thought that . . ."

"Oh, shut up."

His mouth fell open, stunned. "What?" he asked, his voice low, dangerous.

She shifted her weight a little, his cock still buried inside her. It felt spectacular. She cuddled against his chest. "Sometimes I think I hate you," she said softly, her voice low and husky, her accent slightly more pronounced. "And you're right not to trust me. I don't trust you. But I will say, sex with you is . . ." She paused, as if searching for the right words.

"Sex with me is what?" he fished, then clenched his jaw. *Amazing? Mind blowing? Incredible enough to make me forget the crazed, impossible situation we're in?*

Wonderful enough for me to wish we had a different relationship altogether?

"Well," she said bluntly, "it's better when you don't talk afterward."

He couldn't help it. He laughed in shock.

She got up off him, and he felt bereft at the loss of her warmth. She sighed, her expression pragmatic—perhaps a little sad. "You probably know more about sex than I will ever learn, no matter who I sleep with. Everything you do, you do with a purpose." Her clear hazel eyes were unbelievably old for someone so young. "I have no illusions anymore, Dominic."

He hated it, he realized. Hated seeing that wounded look in her eyes. He'd wanted to break her.

Well, now he had.

"So that's it, hmm?" he said, forcing a casual tone. "You're just giving up?"

He waited. She still looked pragmatic . . . but her eyes suddenly flared.

"I'd die first."

The words, said so simply, caused him to grin. He felt his chest warm with something he couldn't recognize.

"Well, before that," he said dryly, getting up and picking up his clothes, "why don't we have dinner?"

She shrugged. "Whatever you want, of course." And there was a ghost of a smile, hovering around her full lips.

He escorted her to the kitchen, still grinning, even as he realized that he was starting to like his enemy, his prisoner, just a little too much.

The redheaded assistant met Jelena at the door of Phillipe's house. This time, she wasn't led to an office, but to a bedroom. It was Las Vegas opulence, something that might be showcased on one of those rich lifestyle programs that Irina was so enamored with. It was a den more than a place to sleep, complete with a fireplace-dominated conversation pit surrounded by pillow-ensconced curved couches, what looked like a small swimming pool, and of course, the requisite enormous bed, covered in peach-colored silk.

Perhaps he'd decided that her ability to get her hands on cash gave her some small modicum of power, she thought. Perhaps she had enough power to tempt him sexually.

She doubted it.

Phillipe stepped out of a side room, looking well dressed as always, although a bit more casual. He wore a charcoal shirt with no tie, and black slacks. He looked like he'd just stepped in from a GQ shoot. He smiled at her.

"Punctual. I appreciate that." He sat down on one of the couches, gesturing to her to do the same. "Now, this should be interesting. How can you teach power? Others have asked me, but never in quite so straightforward a manner."

She wanted to scream at him. She wanted to tear his hair out. *Nadia could be dead by now. Nadia is in trouble, and all you want to do is play these stupid games?*

She knew better. She smiled demurely.

"You said that I'd need power if I were going to save my sister," she murmured. "You said power was more than money. It was determination."

"The willingness to do what others will not," he said, gesturing to his assistant. Silently, she brought him a glass of a dark red wine, then offered the same to Jelena. Jelena turned it down, her stomach knotting. "What are you willing to do, Jelena?"

Jelena frowned. "I've had sex to get money," she said.

"That's not necessarily power." His eyes gleamed over the rim of his wineglass. "That could be simply desperation."

She should have brought a gun, she thought idly. But she got the feeling he was brave enough, and stupid enough, not to back down.

Killing him would not help Nadia any. More's the pity.

She shrugged in response. "It's a step," she conceded. "What would I need to do? To become powerful enough to take down an enemy, and protect what's mine?"

Help me, you supercilious bastard!

He smiled, sipping slowly, as if he knew every second he wasted shredded more of her nerves. "You're right in one thing," he said. "Sex can be a form of power. Can you understand that?"

Jelena closed her eyes, remembering the feel of Robert, pressing against her, his cock plunging inside her. "Yes," she breathed.

She opened her eyes to find Phillipe smiling at her. "Yes, I think you can, now."

He motioned his assistant forward.

"This is April," he said, and her smile was small and sharp, almost mischievous. "I've been mentoring her for a few years now."

Jelena studied the girl. She had a pretty face: appealing, sensitive, rather American. Her hair was a burnished red, full of loose, ringlet curls pulled back in a ponytail. She looked like a grad student. Jelena got the feeling this was a cultivated façade.

April was more than she appeared.

"Perhaps you could instruct Ms. Granville tonight," Phillipe suggested.

April's responding expression was sharp. She walked to Jelena, stroking her shoulder.

Then she knelt in front of Jelena, her smile widening. Up close, Jelena could see April's eyes, a cool, periwinkle violet. There were even a few freckles riding high on the apples of her cheeks, at the corners of her eyes.

April's fingertips brushed the sensitive flesh on the inside of Jelena's wrists, urging her forward. Jelena gasped, looking at Phillipe in surprise and dismay.

His face was completely impassive. He simply sat there, watching.

April moved closer, lifting herself until she was at eye level with Jelena. She moved closer, and Jelena could smell the cinnamon on her breath.

"Am I supposed to . . ." Jelena couldn't even bring herself to finish the sentence. Good grief, what sort of perversity was this? What in the world would this do to help anything?

April shook her head, as if discouraging Jelena from speaking. She leaned forward, her mouth near Jelena's ear. "You've seen it yourself: men like to fuck, and will sacrifice a lot to do so. Women do, too, but we're smarter about it. Sex is a form of power," she said, her voice too husky to be academic, despite the lecturing quality of her speech. "When you know what you like, and know how to perform with someone you'd never expect to, then you'll use sex as a tool and not as a price."

"That makes no sense," Jelena protested, then fell abruptly silent. April's fingertips moved between Jelena's thighs, stroking the inner flesh with a maddening, butterfly-light touch. Jelena swallowed, her heart rate jumping frantically.

"Shhhh." April's fingers delved a little higher, stopping short of Jelena's underwear. She leaned in, her breasts brushing against Jelena's arm. Jelena could feel April's tightened nipples dragging against her.

Jelena sent one last puzzled, frustrated glance over at Phillipe. He smiled smugly.

He wanted her to fail, she realized. This *was* all a game for him.

Something inside her snapped. She felt determination, like her chest was forged from iron.

Jelena stood up, and April followed her. April was shorter, though not by too much. With determination, Jelena leaned down, kissing April gently. To show she would. April's lips were smooth and soft, unexpected after years of kissing men. She pressed forward a bit more insistently. April's tongue moved forward, tracing her lips, slicking over the sensitive inner flesh. Jelena parted her lips, allowing her more easy access. Then she traced her tongue over April's.

April moaned softly with approval, her hands moving forward to gently rest on Jelena's hips, pulling Jelena against her. Jelena felt a tingling awareness between her legs, a little twist in her stomach. She was not repulsed.

Quite the contrary, she realized, and pushed the thought aside.

April pulled away, her violet eyes dilated, her breathing a little bit quicker. Her catlike smile was quick and hungry. She took Jelena's hand, leading her to the giant bed. Phillipe followed, like a ghost, shadowing their progress. Jelena ignored him, keeping her focus on the girl.

This would serve a purpose, Jelena thought. He would continue throwing hoop after hoop at her—to see where she would balk, where she would refuse. When she'd finally gone to the breaking point, he might throw her a bone. Or, he might not.

She stared at April. This woman, though, knew all of Phillipe's plans. Had access to all of his contacts. She was young, and obviously she'd been mindfucked by Phillipe for years. She was malleable. Vulnerable.

She could help me.

Jelena's answering smile at that thought just may have surprised April, because she blinked, her sexual confidence bobbling for the slightest second. Then April regained her composure, moving her hands up, caressing Jelena's breasts. Jelena pushed her chest forward, into April's caress, making a soft moaning noise as April's fingers stroked gently. April smiled more easily now, moving closer, her breasts touching Jelena's as she leaned down to tug up Jelena's skirt, revealing the tops of her stockings and her panties. Nipping at Jelena's collarbone, she maneuvered until she nudged past the elastic of Jelena's underwear, reaching past her curls. She stroked Jelena's clit.

Jelena gasped, involuntarily moving backward, stumbling onto the bed. *Focus, dammit!*

April snickered. In a chair nearby, Phillipe chuckled softly.

"When you fucked to get your money," April said, "did you just lay there, let him do what he liked?"

Jelena felt her cheeks burn. "Not exactly," she hedged, then frowned when April sent her a disbelieving look. "More or less."

"Then he gave you the money because he felt sorry for you, is that it? Because you *begged?*"

"No," Jelena said, realizing it was true. "I seduced him."

April stretched on the bed next to her. "Did you come?"

Jelena shook her head. It had felt good, fucking Robert, but doubted she would have been able to come, given the circumstances. Though for a moment there, she'd really hoped . . .

"You don't need to come every time," April said, "but if you can, why the hell not?"

Jelena grimaced. *Can't we just get on with this, without all the commentary?*

But no . . . April thought she was the master here, especially with Phillipe looking on. This was some sort of test for April as well.

This time, Jelena had to do more than simply get some money from a besotted young fool. April was clever, predatory. It would take more than simply lying back and thinking of her duties to impress this one.

Jelena took a deep breath, anger and adrenaline making her shake. Then she leaned forward. *Coax. Convince. Seduce* . . .

She kissed April more gently this time, her lips barely brushing April's, then she moved out, kissing her jaw, her neck. April sighed with approval. Jelena took it as a sign of encouragement, and reached up. She hadn't handled another woman's breasts before. April had slight breasts, smaller than her own: like apples, high and firm. Jelena kneaded them gently, knowing how much she, herself, hated it when Henry manhandled them in his eagerness. She stroked the nipple, circling it with her thumb. April's sigh was breathier now.

It was easier, Jelena realized, once she focused on what she, herself, enjoyed. If she were to be seduced, she wouldn't want it to be by someone clumsy, or forceful. Though she'd enjoyed the novelty of fucking someone other than Henry, her encounter with her accountant had been exciting mostly because of the thrill of doing something illicit. This had that element, too. The fact that April was a woman added a different sort of taboo.

April moved forward, molding her lips and body against Jelena, and Jelena accepted it, her own breasts tightening, her thighs dampening with anticipation. She hadn't slept with a woman before, but she got the feeling this wouldn't be quite so bad.

In fact, she thought, *this might be amazing.*

April made a little impatient whimper, her hand stroking down, reaching for Jelena's skirt. Jelena reached behind her, undoing the button and zipper, pushing the skirt away. She reached for April's slacks, stripping them off until both women were in blouses and panties. Then Jelena unbuttoned her silk blouse, letting it slip off her shoulders, tossing it to the floor. She tugged April's knit top over her head. April's eyes were low-lidded, and her breathing was uneven as she stared at Jelena expectantly, trying to hold on to her impassive expression. Failing, as her face showed the pleasure that was starting to course through her system.

Jelena felt a little smirk of triumph, and quickly hid it by leaning down, burying her face in April's cleavage. April's nipples jutted against the lace of her cream-colored bra. Jelena took the little hard tip into her mouth, suckling softly, tracing it with her tongue.

April moaned, her back arching, her breast pressing more firmly against Jelena.

Taking her cue, Jelena sucked harder, cupping the other breast in her hand as April's head rolled from side to side.

Then, taking a deep breath, Jelena reached down, pushing her fingers past April's waistband. She met only smooth skin: April was shaved completely nude, her narrow slot already thoroughly damp. Curious and unsettled, Jelena nudged her finger, feeling April's slick knot, already a hard bump against her fingertip. April's short, sharp inhalation switched to a low moan as her hips lifted, nuzzling against Jelena's fingers. Jelena put her fingertips on either side of April's clit, caressing it firmly.

"Yes," April muttered. "God, *yes.*"

Then April nudged her onto her back, taking off Jelena's bra and panties, as well as her own.

April moved her hands against Jelena's breasts caressing them, kissing first one, then the other. Jelena lay frozen, unsure, still not entirely willing, though the sensations drifting through her were building in a way she hadn't felt ever. When April moved between her thighs, Jelena let out a brief, strangled cry of protest. Implacably, April parted her legs, reaching down to the triangle of curls. She pierced them, doing to Jelena what Jelena had done to her. It was the way Jelena liked to touch herself, she realized. She also realized that April did, indeed, know how to touch. Jelena felt her legs relaxing, widening to better accommodate the woman's magical fingers. When April continued to maneuver her clit, she pressed a finger deep inside her at the same time.

Jelena cried out, pleasure overwhelming her.

She was so intent on the sensation that she didn't realize when April leaned her head down, licking her pussy, nibbling delicately on her clit in a way that made Jelena lose her mind. Her hips started to raise off the bed as April suckled, her fingers pressing inside, mimicking a small but agile cock.

Jelena felt heat burning through her like a wildfire. She didn't know she could feel like this—couldn't remember the last time she'd felt anything close. She wanted to give this kind of pleasure. Desire burned her like a torch.

"Wait," she said harshly, her hand buried in April's hair. April looked up, looking disappointed as Jelena started to move her away. But then she looked surprised when Jelena simply changed her position, angling herself so that April was still between her legs. But then, she was also between April's.

She took a deep breath, then stroked the clit that was so close to her, so firm and erect. She spread April's slick folds of skin, and carefully licked the triangular bump.

April cried out, her hips angling forward to give Jelena better access. Jelena sucked more intently, her tongue tracing the hard nubbin of flesh, her fingers moving past, delving deeper inside April. It was so strange, to feel the woman's pussy undulating around her fingers. She tasted like cinnamon and peach.

April quickly delved between Jelena's thighs again, and Jelena's moan was buried against April's cunt. April was obviously more skilled, more experienced, but as she suckled and moved against Jelena, Jelena quickly copied April's every movement. Soon, the two of them were writhing against each other, breasts pressing against stomachs, bodies gyrating as the pleasure intensified exponentially.

Jelena felt the orgasm starting to build inside her, and she pushed her hips more insistently against April's probing tongue. She screamed, her tongue penetrating deep inside, and April's body shuddered in response, her orgasm exploding at the exact same time. Jelena felt like some kind of wild animal, as they shivered and clung to each other, pleasure shooting through them like electricity.

After long moments, they rolled away from each other. Jelena moved so her head rested on a pillow, and April rested next to her shoulder, looking a little dazed. She hadn't expected things to turn out this way, apparently.

Neither, for that matter, had Jelena.

Phillipe hovered over them, blocking the light. "Impressive," he said, his voice casual, even as Jelena noticed the raging hard-on in his black slacks. "I'll get you both towels, something to drink." He smirked. "The night's young, after all. Perhaps you'll have some more lessons to learn."

Jelena waited until he left the room, heading for a bathroom nearby. She cuddled against April, who after a moment's stiffness, melted against Jelena.

"I need your help," Jelena murmured, so close to April's ear that she doubted any tape could pick it up. "Will you see me? Away from here?"

April's eyes looked wary.

Jelena pressed soft kisses against her collarbone, sweetly, while stroking April's breast. April shuddered, her thigh covering Jelena's, her hips swiveling slightly, insistently.

"All right," she whispered against Jelena's lips, kissing her again.

Jelena held her tight in gratitude, kissing her. Then felt some shivering again in the pit of her stomach, as the kiss grew more intent.

"Now, now, ladies," she heard Phillipe say. "At least let me get some popcorn."

Jelena growled against April's lips.

If you think this is a show, she thought fiercely, as she pressed against April's body, *wait till you see what I've got coming up.*

Chapter Six

Find something to use against him.

Nadia wasn't sure if she was looking for a weapon, or for something less tangible: maybe information? Although she doubted she would be able to find anything that would be useful to blackmail him with. After all, she was a prisoner here. Who was she going to tell? Even if she escaped, she doubted she was strong enough to stay away from him for long.

Especially since, with every passing day, she seemed to grow more and more addicted to him.

She didn't know how it was happening. Stockholm syndrome, perhaps, that bizarre dysfunction where captives became dependent on their captors. Was she losing herself, then?

She sighed. It might be easier if he weren't such a damned good lover.

The "punishments" had not stopped, but they were no longer menacing. They were strangely ritualistic. If she were the slightest bit uncomfortable, he seemed able to sense it, and quickly changed the scenario to better accommodate her. Last night, he'd handcuffed her to the banister of the curving stairs, going down on her as she writhed, unable to move. But when he'd seen that the cuffs were biting into her wrists, he'd quickly changed the binding to soft silk cloths. And she'd stood there, rubbing at her wrists . . . waiting for him to return. She'd actually lifted her arms, holding still so he could secure her in place before continuing his sensual torment.

He wasn't trying to hurt her. He was trying to pleasure her. And it was working more than she'd ever dreamed.

She supposed it should have been demeaning, strutting around a man's house completely nude, awaiting his orders, making herself available to his every whim. But what happened when your body started *craving* those whims? When you found yourself going out of your way to make sure he'd be around? When you started pretending defiance, rather than expressing the anger you knew you righteously deserved to display?

What was she supposed to do when she was starting to enjoy the game?

She explored the house instead. He rarely left the mansion— the fortress, to be more accurate—so now that she was alone and not locked in her room, she took the opportunity. Maybe she'd find something to answer the questions that were beginning to plague her, more and more.

Maybe, just maybe, she'd find a way out, literally and figuratively.

She went down the hallway that led to her bedroom. Grimly, she tried every door. Most of them were locked. She turned the handle on one, and when it opened, she entered cautiously.

It was a home theater, in the true sense of the word, like those owned by all those stars on *Cribs* or *Lifestyles of the Rich and Famous* or any of the other reality shows her sister Irina watched so intently had. There were eight very plush seats, a large screen, and discreet but obviously high-tech speakers. Built-in bookcases covered the back wall beneath the projector, stocked full of high-definition DVDs. She glanced over the titles absently. There were typical guy flicks: *300, Gladiator, Die Hard.* Any number of mindless action movies that even she enjoyed from time to time. A lot of noir-styled movies with anti-heroes, she noticed: *The Maltese Falcon, Casablanca, L.A. Confidential. The Usual Suspects. Chinatown.*

Depressing, she thought. So it was either blood-and-guts or criminal despair. It suited what she knew about him. She had to be crazy to feel anything for such a . . .

Her eyes narrowed as she got to the lowest corner of the bookshelf.

"Cartoons?" she murmured in surprise, tracing her finger over the covers. *The Incredibles. 101 Dalmations. Shrek. Kung Fu Panda.*

She heard a noise, and abruptly stood, her heart racing.

It came from the door she'd left open. More specifically, it came from the far end of the hallway.

"Dominic?" she called softly. Would he be angry, finding her nosing about in his rooms?

What would he do?

It wasn't fear, she realized. It was excitement.

She ignored that discovery, focusing instead on what she was hearing. It was a soft clicking sound, vaguely familiar. It was followed by a sound like heavy breathing, coming from a large set of double doors at the far end of the hallway. She instantly realized: these were the doors to Dominic's suite. A man like Dominic would have another exit, just in case.

If there was a way out, it'd be through these doors.

"Hello?" she tried again, walking to the doors and knocking softly. Of course, the doors would be locked. Who knew what else . . .

She heard a low animal growl.

It was unlocked, twisting easily in her palm. She started to turn the handle. She opened the door.

She got a glimpse of dark wood paneling and high vaulted ceilings, with dim, recessed lights. Then, snarling white teeth appeared at the door.

Shrieking, she slammed the door shut. Loud, deep, angry barking was barely muffled by the door. Falling on her butt, she scooted a few feet away.

"I see you've met Max," Dominic said drily behind her.

She squeaked, spinning.

Dominic looked haggard, his complexion a bit ashy. His

blue eyes were slightly unfocused. "That would be my dog," Dominic explained. His voice sounded tired. "He makes sure that no one invades my privacy."

"I was just . . ."

"I'm sure." Dominic's smile was wrong. He wasn't angry. It was like he barely noticed she was there. "I'll punish you later. Go on. Go to your room, wait for me."

It was then that she realized he was holding his side. Without thinking, she tugged open his jacket. There, just beneath his gun holster, was a deep, bloody gash.

"Oh, my God." She paled. "What happened?"

"Nothing," he growled, more with irritation than anger. "Just leave, Nadia."

"This is serious!" She looked at him like he was insane. "You should go to a hospital!"

"Stop," he said. Now there was anger. "I can take care of this. Hell, I've had worse than this. Get the hell away from me, will you?"

"You're going to stitch this up yourself?"

He shrugged. "If it needs it."

"You look like you're going to pass out on your feet," she protested. "Here, I'll take care of it."

"Oh, really?" he drawled.

"I trained to be a nurse in Moscow," she muttered. "I didn't like it, but I'm not bad at it."

He still looked skeptical.

"Besides, I'd get to see you in pain as I pushed a needle into you," she said, rolling her eyes.

He sighed. "Good point."

Then he collapsed partly against her, and she propped him up as best she could. Really worried now. He was more hurt than he let on.

She opened the door. The dog was there, still snarling, until Dominic said "Max," in an exasperated tone. She stared. It was some kind of pit bull mix, she thought . . . perhaps Labrador. She'd always liked Labradors. It went quiet, growling low in its throat, looking at her suspiciously. Then it sniffed at Dominic, letting out a little whine.

"Get me on my bed," Dominic said, "then give him a treat from the side of the bed, will you? Otherwise, he'll be a pain in the ass, and I don't want him biting you."

She did as instructed, quailing slightly. Dogs. She'd been afraid of dogs. "Here, doggy . . . Max," she remembered. She held out the biscuit.

The dog snapped at her. Squealing, she dropped the thing. Max devoured it in a second. Then he sat, tongue lolling out, looking at her expectantly.

"Should I give him another?" she asked quietly.

"Hell, no," Dominic said, closing his eyes. "I spoil him enough."

She sighed. She helped Dominic take his jacket off. When she reached for his gun, he stopped her.

"I may be hurt," he said softly, "but I'm not stupid."

She nodded, feeling a little encouraged . . . and a little disappointed. "Where is your first aid kit?"

"In the bathroom," he said, taking off the holster awkwardly, then putting the gun in his uninjured hand. She retrieved a well-stocked box, pulling out what she'd need. Her hands didn't shake, and she felt remarkably calm as she got the needle ready. She stripped off his shirt, examining the gash clinically.

"Knife?" she asked.

He nodded.

"Argument?" She cleaned the wound, thinking to keep him talking. He didn't seem to have anything resembling anesthetic, so this was going to hurt.

"Not exactly," he said, not even wincing as the needle pierced his skin. He remained perfectly still, even though his grip on his gun tightened. "Listen, I don't want to talk about it."

"You should take a painkiller," she said, then rolled her eyes when he shook his head. "Fine." She rummaged in the kit, pouring out a few pills. "Then at least take the antibiotics."

He scowled at her, then took the pills. She grinned to herself, and he didn't notice. She started to work on the wound again. He grew a little more pale, his forehead sweating slightly.

"You know, talking might take your mind off the pain," she suggested.

"It's fine." He looked stoic.

She yanked on the thread. He hissed, glaring at her, moving the gun with meaning. She smirked back at him. "Read any good books lately?"

He stared for a second, then relaxed slightly—as much as he could, she supposed. "Not really. But I've acquired a new hobby I'm enjoying."

A hobby. Was that what she was to him?

And what the hell is he to you?

She saw his eyes start to glaze slightly. It wasn't blood loss—he was right, it looked worse than it was, although she felt sure it hurt like hell. Of course, she'd slipped the pain-killer alongside the antibiotic. He was too busy glaring at her to look. Which meant that he was in enough pain to be tricked.

She ought to feel more triumphant. Instead, she felt . . .

Good God. Am I actually worried about him?

She froze.

"Are you almost done?" he asked irritably, snapping her out of it.

"So," she said, her voice shaking, "you were randomly stabbed. I guess that's why you don't leave the house very often."

"I seem to remember saying I don't want to talk about it," he muttered, but his voice sounded sleepy. "It wasn't random, though. And yes, it is the reason I don't leave the house very often." He grinned. "That, and because I don't like being too far from your delicious naked body."

She felt a little tug of desire, and frowned at him. "You're not in any state for that," she scolded gently, even as the flesh between her legs twitched expectantly.

"My cock would differ with you," he said, and she noticed that he did, indeed, have an erection. "But you're probably right. Wouldn't want to tear these stitches, huh?" He leaned back, sighing. "I hate stitches. Hate hospitals."

"Because of . . ." She paused, wondering if maybe she'd gone too far.

"The explosion, you mean." He was slurring a little. "Yeah. I was lucky—if Alexis had known about the guy I went to, she would've paid him to kill me when I was under the anesthetic. She's still got a hit out on me."

"Alexis?" Nadia asked blankly. Who was that?

And why are you jealous?

"Old girlfriend," he said. "Old lover, really. She thought we were going to get married. Got pretty pissed when she found out I was still playing the field."

"You cheated on her?" Nadia tied off the stitches, bandaging the wound.

He sighed. "I was a different guy then," Dominic said. "And Alexis was special."

"Oh." Bile rose in Nadia's throat. "You're all taken care of . . ."

To her surprise, Dominic reached out, took her hand. "Alexis was the daughter of the man I admired most on earth," he said carefully, opening his eyes to look at her. "If he wanted me to marry her, then I would have. She was beautiful, and amazing. But she was cruel, and utterly spoiled. Whatever she wanted, she got."

"Oh," Nadia repeated, this time with different inflection. Dominic didn't sound like himself. There was no sarcasm, no coyness. He was being completely honest.

"So she decided she wanted to own me," he said, and he stroked the back of her palm. "Of course, she still had other lovers, too. But *nobody* screwed around on Alexis Carmello. I guess it totally humiliated her. And she really thought she was in love with me."

"What happened?" Nadia breathed.

She'd never seen the naked pain in his eyes before. It seared her to her soul.

"Once her father died," he said, "I left the organization. And she took the opportunity to try and kill me."

Nadia swallowed hard.

"It didn't work, obviously," he said, his voice thick. "But it left me like this."

She clutched his hand, hard. She wanted to kiss the pain away. There weren't enough kisses in the world.

"I wasn't always like this," he murmured, then drifted off into sleep.

She froze, listening to his deep, even breathing. Even his dog was lying at the foot of the bed, completely relaxed.

Take the gun. Kill him. Get his car and get the hell out of here. Nobody would find him. Nobody would know it was her . . .

She stared, his scarred face defenseless in sleep. His grip had relaxed, the gun slipping from his palm. She picked it up carefully.

Then, just as carefully, she placed it on the nightstand. She took off his shoes, then pulled a light throw over his bare chest. Carefully, she sat at the edge of the bed.

She couldn't do it. He'd had so many chances to kill her, and he hadn't. He'd played with her: he'd introduced her to her body, to pleasure, to a whole different side of herself. Call it Stockholm syndrome, or dysfunction, or sheer insanity. But she couldn't kill him while he slept.

She left the room, going to the kitchen, making herself a cup of tea. Then she went to his library, examining his books. She found a mystery writer she liked, and settled down in one of the chairs by his bed, reading quietly.

He woke with a start, reaching around the bed for his gun, yelling. Then he focused.

"You drugged me," he said. "You fucking *drugged* me!"

She clucked her tongue. "You needed to rest."

He took the gun, his face livid. *"You drugged me!"*

She closed the book. "And I put your gun on the night-stand."

He stared at her, not comprehending. Then he stood up. "Go to your room."

"Of course," she said, but it held none of their usual banter. She was genuinely worried about him. Which only spoke to her insanity.

Two days later, he'd only said the barest of words to her. She was really worried now. *What was he going to do?* She'd thought of asking him how he would punish her, but she got the feeling it wasn't that kind of game. Not anymore.

On the third day, he finally walked up to her. He tossed her a bundle of clothes. They were clean, the jeans and T-shirt and simple underwear she'd worn the first night he'd brought her here. Even her sneakers.

"Get dressed," he said sharply.

"Dressed?" she echoed nervously. He didn't look play-ful, or angry, now. She couldn't make out *how* he felt. "Why? What are you going to do with me?"

He looked determined. And in agony.

She felt fear, cold and overwhelming.

"Nadia," he said softly. "I'm taking you back."

Dominic told himself he was just trying to drive carefully, not bring any attention to himself, especially after the last attack on him down at that bar. But the truth was, he'd never driven this slowly. He was handling the Lexus like he was a little old woman, for God's sake.

You need to let her go.

He grimaced, his hands tightening on the leather of the steering wheel until he saw the bone of his knuckles through his skin. He shot a quick glance at Nadia. She was wringing her hands, staring out the window. She looked paler than usual.

"I'd think this would make you happy," he growled, and then cursed himself.

"What would make me happy?"

"Going home." *Getting away from me.*

She finally looked at him, hazel eyes lost, wounded. "Why are you taking me back?" she whispered. "What did I do wrong?"

Do wrong?

"You drugged me."

"I could have killed you," she pointed out. "I didn't. I took care of you."

"I know."

And that was precisely why he needed to let her go.

They drove in silence for a while longer, and finally she said, "Are you going to kill my family, then? And me?"

"What?" He didn't mean to yell, and he hated watching her cringe away from him. He forced himself to lower his voice. "What the hell? No, I'm not killing them *or* you. I'm not killing anyone. I'm just . . ." He paused. "You know. Returning you."

God, that sounded like shit.

"Oh." She didn't look more pleased with that.

"I swear. I'm not going to hurt anyone."

"All right."

He gritted his teeth. "Jesus, Nadia, what do you want from me?" he muttered. She frowned at that, but didn't respond. "You'll be back with your family. Maybe you can get a normal life . . . you know. The husband, all that."

Even as he said it, the words were distasteful. He didn't like the idea of Nadia belonging to anyone else, much less whatever rich scumbag her father would probably pick out for her. Hell, he'd probably be doing her a favor by keeping her.

But what would she do to you?

She'd taken care of him. She'd tended his wound. Yes, she'd drugged him—but instead of using his vulnerability to attack him, she'd made sure he was all right. She'd kept watch over him. No one had ever taken care of him, for as long as he could remember. Sex had always been a conquest—either on his part, or the part of the woman seducing him. He'd never gotten close enough to feel he could open up to someone, and now, thanks to a stupid Vicodin, he'd found himself babbling about his past to a woman that could have blown his brains out. The fact that she hadn't made him wonder what it would be like to open up to her even more.

That was the problem.

The more he kept her with him, the more he found himself wanting. If this kept up, he'd not only be vulnerable, he'd be hopelessly, futilely in love with her. And that would be dangerous for both of them.

What the hell did a man like him have to offer to anyone, much less a noble, passionate, vibrant woman like Nadia?

No. He'd shove her back into the bosom of her family, and let her go. That was the right thing to do. The smart thing.

They pulled off the freeway onto the main roads of Las Vegas. She cleared her throat. "You're going to want to turn right . . ."

"I remember," he said curtly, then sighed when she fell silent yet again. He wove through the streets easily, coming to a stop at the dingy apartment complex. He looked carefully: he knew he hadn't been followed, doubted that any thugs from the last ill-conceived attempt would have followed him. He'd been sloppy, going to that bar to try and get away from his growing obsession for Nadia, and had missed the cues when the stupid thugs had entered. If he hadn't had Nadia on his mind, he never would've gotten clipped, barely getting out with the stupid, small scratch.

She was making him vulnerable in more ways than one.

Still cursing himself, he moved protectively toward her car door, standing close to her as he scanned the walkways and rooftops.

"You can just leave me here, on the sidewalk," she said. Her voice was low, almost inaudible.

He should, he realized. But then it would really be over,

and his whole body recoiled at the thought. "That wouldn't be very gentlemanly of me, would it?" he said instead, putting off the inevitable for a few moments more.

She shot him a wry, sad look. "Of course. I forgot. You're such a gentleman." For a split second, she leaned against his arm.

The wave of regret and passion almost drove him to his knees. He grimaced, then nudged her forward. "Maybe I'll have a little talk with your father, as long as I'm here." *And make sure that if that old bastard tries to barter her off to anyone, I'll be really unhappy.*

She looked nervously at him. "Why?"

"I already told you, I'm not going to kill him," he said, then saw her little grimace. "Okay. I won't hurt him, either."

She relaxed visibly. He was irritated that she'd immediately jump to the thought he'd be violent . . . then realized that, in any other circumstance, she'd probably be right. Besides, as soon as he said differently, she instantly believed him.

When was the last time anyone trusted him?

"I just want to see if he's had any luck with my goddamned car," he said instead.

"You never did tell me why it's so important," she said, as they walked toward the apartment. "Your personal reasons."

"I think I've told you plenty of personal things lately."

She accepted the rebuke, her shoulders hunching slightly.

He took a deep breath. What was one more secret, especially now? It wasn't like it could hurt him.

"It belonged to a guy I knew, once. A man who was really important to me. He gave it to me just before he died."

"Alexis's father," she surmised.

Just the thought made his throat tight. He nodded.

"I'm so sorry," she breathed, putting a hand on his arm.

He shrugged, then surprised himself by continuing. "He said he wanted his son to have it, but I was the closest thing he had to one, so . . ."

She nodded, not saying anything.

Dominic cleared his throat. It was so easy, telling her stuff. So damned easy. He had to get rid of her, quickly, or God knows what he'd turn into.

They got to the door, and she knocked. When he looked at her quizzically, she sent him a crooked little half-smile.

"I left so quickly last time," she clarified, "I didn't have my keys or purse, or anything."

When you took her, she means. Dominic stared fiercely at the door. No one answered. She knocked harder, cursing softly in Russian under her breath.

"You lookin' for me, pretty?"

Dominic turned, his hand already reaching for his gun. It was a man, short, his head closely shaved, wearing a wife-beater tank top. His arms sported tattoos from shoulder to wrist. He sent Nadia a cheesy you-know-you-want-me look, sheer pointless bravado.

Dominic took a step between her and the little guy. "Who the hell are you?" Dominic said, his voice low and lethal.

Short Guy took in Dominic's imposing appearance. The slick smile quickly evaporated. "Hey, man, that's my door she's knockin' on. I'm not trying to start nothing."

"Your door?" Nadia asked.

"Just moved in," he said, not taking a step closer. He kept shooting nervous glances at Dominic. "Landlord said the last family moved out in a hurry. If you're looking for them, hey, I don't even know them. Never met, and don't want any trouble, got it?"

"No," Dominic said. "No trouble."

"They just . . . left?"

Nadia sounded stunned. Bereft. She leaned against Dominic unconsciously, and it was all he could do not to envelope her in his arms and bring her back to the car.

Instead, he noted clinically: "They just vanished. Didn't expect you to ever come back."

"It's not like they could send me a forward address," she said sharply, but he could see the way her mind was racing. She was probably busy trying to justify what they'd done. The bottom line was, their first thought had been to cover their own asses, and screw whatever happened to Nadia.

Dominic felt anger at their betrayal on her behalf.

"They abandoned you," he snarled.

"No," she corrected quickly. "My stepmother is pregnant. My father was keeping her and the baby safe. For all they knew, you were going to come back and kill them."

Now the bald-headed guy was holding his hands up, backing away. "Definitely don't want any trouble," he muttered. "You just work your shit out. I'll come back later." He bolted.

Dominic was quiet for a moment, then he cleared his throat. "What do you think you'll do now?"

She bit her full lower lip. He wanted to do the same, to her. "I'll think of something."

"You don't have any cash," he reminded her.

"I'll call . . . my sister. Jelena," she finally said, even though her brow still furrowed slightly.

"You don't have a cell."

"I'll call collect," she said stubbornly.

"And what will happen when you call her?" he said, in what he thought was a logical tone of voice. "You're going to tell her that you need help? That the big bad Beast is done with you?"

"What do you care?" she snapped. "You're the one who's getting rid of me!"

He smiled. "No, I don't think so. Not now."

"What?" She looked floored.

He grabbed her arm, relief singing through him like a choir. "Bringing you back was a mistake, obviously. Your family only looks out for number one . . . except for you, anyway. You've got the survival instincts of a lemming, for Christ's sake."

"So you're, what? Saving me?" she said, yanking her arm away from him. "You *pity* me now?"

"Nadia . . ."

"*Fuck you!*" She started to stomp away, and he grabbed her, pulling her to him hard. His side screamed, his stitches straining.

"I don't fucking pity you," he whispered sharply in her ear, holding her captive. "I can't describe what I feel for you, but trust me, pity isn't it."

She melted against him, resistance and anger replaced with

a tender confusion. "Then why?" She gestured at the dingy apartment complex. "Why bring me back here at all?"

He took a deep breath.

What can I tell her? That I can't breathe without wanting her? That the fact that she trusts me makes me want to never let her go? That I'm afraid of losing her? That I'm afraid of her hating me?

Nothing. He couldn't tell her anything at all.

Instead, he kissed her, hard. She wrapped her arms around his neck, pulling herself tight against him. When he finally pulled away, she was still expectant.

"Stop asking questions."

He took her back to the car. She remained silent the entire ride home, although the question—*why did you try to get rid of me, only to keep me?*—still hung in the air. Tension sang through his muscles, and his side ached. He could feel her gaze on his features, not in the grotesque, sideshow staring way that most indulged in. It was as if she were *willing* him to answer her question.

"Stop staring at me," he said finally, unable to handle the sensation of it.

"No."

He turned away from the road to look at her, head on. She didn't wince, didn't waver. Her eyes were bright, beautiful.

"Fine. Look all you damned well want."

He drove like a demon, and they got back to his house in record time, nothing like the first portion of this little joy-ride. He drove up to the gates with a barely held impatience, his body getting more and more tense.

More aroused.

She would still be there. He wasn't doing the smart thing, definitely wasn't doing the right thing. *But she would still be there.*

He pulled into the garage, killing the engine, getting out. He walked around the car, opening her door for her. He expected her to lay into him: interrogate him, or maybe offer him more justifications for her family's cowardice.

Instead, she jumped for him, clamping her hands onto his shoulders, kissing him with all the confusion and passion and frustration, all the sadness and anger, every emotion roiling through her system. He could taste her tears as well as feel the heat of her, practically singeing him.

He groaned in response, crushing her against the side of his car. His stitches were probably torn to hell and gone, but he didn't care. His mouth never left hers as he kissed her fiercely, savoring her taste, needing to feel her, reassuring himself that she was still there and still his and she wasn't going anywhere.

He reached down, and he felt her hands there, helping him, fumbling with his belt, undoing his fly before tearing at her own. She was wearing the jeans she'd worn the night he brought her here. She scratched her skin in her haste, tearing off her jeans. He yanked down his pants and reached for her hips, bringing her up against him, guiding her legs around his waist as he positioned his cock at her warm, wet opening. Before he could breathe, he plunged inside her, roaring with the pleasure and the relief of the wash of sensations.

It was fast, insanely fast. He felt her pussy shiver against the hot flesh of his cock, suckling him, squeezing him. She clutched at him, driving her hips against his, her thighs clenching tightly at his pelvis. She kissed him like a woman possessed as he pumped against her, rocking against the hard, hot metal of the car beneath them. She made mewling noises of pleasure, her breathing choppy and harsh, crying out in pain and passion as he drove himself inside her. She bit his lower lip gently, and he swept his tongue forward, mating it with hers. His hips pistoned against hers, wanting to get closer to her, as close as humanly possible.

She punctuated her first orgasm with a scream against his lips, her nails scratching against the fabric of his jacket. She was still trembling and clutching against him when his orgasm tore through him. His hips shook and rattled as the hot spurt of cum burst inside her, filling her.

He collapsed, having only the sense to turn, cradling her against him as he breathed hard, pulling her away from the car before he crushed her. Holding her tightly, he found himself stroking her hair, pressing hot, soft kisses against the crown of her head.

In that moment, he realized: he was keeping her. No matter what. Her family didn't know what they'd given up, but he did. He knew what he'd almost lost.

If he just kept her here, hidden from his past, hidden from the world . . . maybe, just maybe, he'd have a chance at keeping her.

Chapter Seven

"Jelena! Get the fuck down here, right now!"

Jelena paused in the act of dialing her cell phone, feeling a wave of irritation. She was supposed to be talking to April, who said a few days earlier that she was going to get the name of a contact . . . someone who was an archenemy of Dominic Luder's, who might be open to some kind of a bargain.

Hearing her husband's voice was the last thing she needed. Any other moment, she'd already be off the seat at her dressing table and halfway down the stairs, to the foyer where her husband was yelling. Her stomach would be in sickly knots; her palms would be sweating as her mind raced through a list of what she may have done wrong, and how best she could rectify the situation.

Now, she remained at her dressing table. Taking a deep

breath, she wiped her hands discreetly on a small towel, then touched up her makeup.

She saw his livid reflection in her mirror. "Didn't you hear me?" he bellowed.

"Hard not to," she murmured, slicking some lip gloss on her lips.

He grabbed her shoulder, painfully, forcing her to her feet. Adrenaline shot through her.

"The money, Jelena," he said, his voice pitched high and squeaky in his anger. "Did you think I wouldn't find out about the goddamned money?"

She'd always focused on the emotion before, she realized, and her own fear. Now it was like she was watching a television show. Had he always sounded so effeminate in his rage?

"Answer me!"

Her stomach calmed. Her jaw clenched. "Of course I knew you'd find out about the money," she said crisply.

For a second, he looked surprised, and it threw him off stride. His fingers tightened on her shoulder, painfully. "What did you do with it?"

"I need to help my family." Now the words were raw with emotion. "You wouldn't help me."

"So you decided to just take my money?" His laugh was cruel, sarcastic. "Man, you make it easy. I'm divorcing you."

"Of course you are." Her voice matched his, tone for tone. "Like I'd keep you."

Again, a flash of surprise. "I'm kicking your ass out with nothing," he said. "I'll give you five minutes. And take those fucking diamonds off your neck. You're not leaving this house with a penny."

She crossed her arms, feeling a cold calm surround her, like a coat of ice. "I don't think so."

He reached for the necklace, his fingers grazing her throat painfully.

Before she knew what she was going to do, her foot sprang out, catching him hard in the groin. He went pale, then red, spluttering and gripping himself as he fell onto the carpet.

She'd never felt such a surge of pure, violent power before. She towered over him, tempted to kick him in the face. "Let me tell you what I did with *your* money, Henry," she murmured. "I hired a private detective, a good one. I've got pictures of you with an assortment of various women. And I use the term lightly, since there's that one whose age seems a little questionable."

He gurgled at her, his eyes bugging in a rage.

"And that one man," she added casually. "Oh, and a good accountant friend of mine went over your company's books, did I mention? I'm sure the IRS would be happy to see what you've been up to, at the very least."

"You . . . you . . ."

"Besides, some of those clients of yours . . ." She clucked her tongue. "I'm sure that if they realized the kind of information you were collecting on them, willing to blackmail them or double-cross them . . . If someone were to tell them what you'd been up to, I imagine jail would be the least of your worries."

He stopped thrashing around, staring at her with mute horror from the floor.

She stood in front of him, feeling like a giant about to squash a particularly pesky bug. She couldn't believe she'd ever been afraid of him. Couldn't believe the lengths she'd gone to try and please him. She must have been insane.

"Here's how this plays out," she said. "You'll move out of this house, today. We will get divorced, but you're going to give me one of the most generous settlements they've ever seen in Nevada. In exchange, you're going to get to live a free man."

His eyes narrowed with pure fury.

"And before you get any bright ideas," she added calmly, feeling a pleasant viciousness curl through her, "if anything happens to me, I've got people who will make sure that everything I just warned you about will happen. You'll die, either in jail or out of it, and probably very, very painfully."

Slowly, he stood up. She studied him. His shoulders slumped: his expression was bewildered, like a bully who'd just gotten his first real ass-kicking. She didn't turn her back on him. She wouldn't, ever again.

If he were smart, he would do the same with her. Then again, he hadn't been smart.

He shook his head. "I didn't think you were capable of this."

She shrugged delicately, still staring at him.

"If I'd known . . ." He continued his head-shaking, a cross between incredulity and disdain. "No man would ever *touch* a bitch like you, much less marry one."

She kept her arms crossed carefully.

"I can find another stupid little bitch in less than half an hour. More beautiful than you. Younger. Willing to do whatever the fuck I want her to. But you? You're damaged. Used. *Old*," he emphasized. "Don't you understand that? No man's going to have you."

She smiled. At one time, that would have been the worst curse she could have imagined. She would have been paralyzed with the fear of it, trying to whatever she could to mitigate the situation.

Now?

"You are damned right about that," she breathed. "No man's ever going to 'have' me again. Now get out of *my* house." She bared her teeth in a smile that was barely human. "I've got better things to do."

She left him there, whimpering and puffing, and picked up her cell phone, dialing April's number.

"Can you talk?" she asked, when April picked up.

April paused for a second. "Yes. He's not here." *He* being Phillipe. "I did a little research. There's a woman, a really high-powered woman. Daughter of an old mafia don, apparently. Alexis Carmello. Owns a really ritzy brothel, for women clientele."

"How can I contact her?"

"She's really hard to get a hold of," April hedged. "But she's going to be at a party tonight." April's voice lowered. "I got ahold of an invitation."

Jelena wanted to crow, triumphantly. "Wonderful. I'll be there to pick it up." She lowered her voice. "Perhaps I'll stay for a little bit."

"I'd like that," April murmured, and Jelena's stomach twitched in anticipation. *You're just using her*, she reminded herself.

Henry groaned loudly. Jelena sighed.

"Give me half an hour to throw out some trash, and I'll be there."

I need to know more about him.

Dominic was recovering nicely, and things had settled into their usual routine—if anything they did could be considered "usual." They'd pulled some of his stitches when they'd had sex so frantically in the garage. She'd tried to insist that he be more careful, even as she felt like a fool when she did. He smiled at her, an endearing, gentle smile that warmed her in a way all the blazing sex in the world couldn't. He'd even slept in her bed in the guest suite, a first for them. Of course, they'd spent several hours making very thorough, albeit gentle, love up to that point.

She closed her eyes. Yes, she reassured herself, they'd made love. Or at least, she had.

She couldn't deny it anymore. Whether it was illusion or a product of stress or whatever, she was falling in love with Dominic Luder. Maybe it was the biggest foolishness in the world; maybe it was a mistake that would cost her her life, she didn't know. But she knew now that no one was as tender or as caring, no one listened to her, and no one seemed to know her as well as Dominic did.

If only she knew more about him, and could lay some of these nagging concerns to rest . . .

He'd left for the day, promising her he'd be careful. He was going to see the doctor he trusted, to make sure the stitches were really okay, and to get a refill on antibiotics. She'd insisted, partially because she truly was concerned about him—but also because she really wanted him out of the house.

In the panic of his injury, she hadn't really had the time to investigate his bedroom suite, but she'd remembered there were other rooms there besides the bedroom. His suite was his sanctum. If she were going to find out more about him, then surely that would be the place.

Once she watched his car leave the driveway and the gate close behind it, she went to the suite. She opened the door, bracing herself for Max's violent snarls.

"It's just me," she said firmly, trying not to be afraid. Didn't all the clichés say that dogs always smelled fear? She probably smelled drenched in it. He growled at her, then barked once, twice, in a clear warning.

She stepped past him. "Easy, Max."

He curled his lip, displaying a few large, obviously sharp white teeth. His growl grew louder, more intent.

She walked quickly to the side of the bed, her hand trembling slightly as she reached in for a dog biscuit. She held it out.

The snarl ceased abruptly. He still looked suspicious, but she saw his tail starting to wag traitorously.

"Sit," she commanded.

He shot her a you've-got-to-be-kidding-me look.

"All right, don't sit," she said, tossing him the treat. He

caught it in midair, and was already chewing it before his feet touched the ground again. He munched happily, tail in full swing. "I'll give you one more if you stop barking at me."

He walked up to her, and she held out one more biscuit on her flat open palm. But instead, he sniffed her fingertips, her wrist. He must smell Dominic, she realized. Then he quickly snatched the other biscuit, gobbling it up. He nudged her hand with his broad, flat head, then licked away crumbs. Smiling a little, she patted his head cautiously. He moved to ensure she turned it into a stroke. Pretty soon, she was stroking his head and scratching behind his ears as his tail wagged furiously.

As she paid attention to Max, she surveyed the bedroom suite. It was cavernous, dark, just as she'd remembered it. He didn't pay very much attention to it: the bed wasn't made, clothes were strewn near a chair. It wasn't like the rest of the house at all. There were three other rooms. One, she knew, was the bathroom, where she'd gotten the medical kit.

Somewhere in the other two were the answers she wanted.

When Max was finally satisfied, moving to his bed next to the bedroom's fireplace—apparently, Dominic loved fireplaces—she moved carefully to the first closed door. Taking a deep breath, she opened it.

She didn't understand what she was looking at, at first. There was a large dog bed, and a mountain of half-chewed toys. Exploring a little more, she found some cupboards that held various treats, brushes, soaps, and medicines. The water in the sterling-silver dog bowl was automatically refreshed.

Max followed her, his tongue lolling out as he gave her a

canine grin. He bounded inside, jumping on a large hunk of rope and tugging it across the floor.

"You have your own room?" she asked, stunned. In answer, Max rolled happily, grabbing up a toy and shaking it vigorously.

She started laughing. Of course Max had his own room. He was Dominic's closest friend.

Still smiling, she walked to the other room. Stepping inside, she found an office, of sorts: a large desk with an expensive-looking glossy black computer, complete with three widescreen monitors. Over against one wall, there was a bank of television screens. She frowned, looking closer. No, not televisions: security screens, closed circuit, obviously. After a second, she recognized the rooms each screen displayed—the kitchen, the living room, all as seen from above. Obviously there were hidden cameras in the ceiling, carefully camouflaged. She recognized the view in her bedroom. He had the whole place under surveillance.

It didn't surprise her. It didn't even really disturb her. She traced her fingers over the screen that showed her bed.

I wonder if he keeps tapes.

She felt the heat of a blush at the thought, but still enjoyed the pervasive, curious heat. Still, that wasn't why she was there. She ignored the distraction, moving past the surveillance equipment to the large desk instead.

She wasn't sure what she was looking for. She flipped past folders in his desk drawers: miscellaneous bank accounts, financial holdings, contracts. She didn't care about that. Each subsequent drawer seemed to produce more of the same.

Irritated, she closed the last drawer. What had she expected to find? A folder, neatly labeled "my past," waiting for her or anyone rifling through his room to discover it?

She frowned, then turned on his computer, going onto the Internet. He had a miraculously fast internet connection. She did some Google searches, looking through news archives. There were plenty from several years ago. Lots of arrests, few convictions. Then she searched for images.

The picture of him took her breath away.

He was beautiful, in a purely masculine, awe-inspiring way. He had a sensual, gorgeous face that really could have been called angelic were it not for the promise of violence and power in his eyes. Even in the dull two dimensions of a monitor, he looked seductive. Several of the images were of him with equally beautiful women—sometimes several at one time. Jealousy struck her, fast and hard, and she quickly clicked away from those pictures, although there seemed to be hundreds. Finally, she stopped quickly as she saw a caption that made her freeze:

"Dominic Luder with mob daughter Alexis Carmello."

She stared at the woman in the picture. She was stunning, like some kind of Amazon princess. She had an arm through Dominic's, but her smile was one of smug possession as she surveyed the crowd around them. It was at some society party, and the woman was dripping with diamonds. But Dominic wasn't staring at her with adoration, as most of the others were. He looked uncomfortable, his eyes directed away from her, his expression bored.

It was a start . . . but it wasn't enough.

"Wanted to check your e-mail, huh?"

She sighed, then turned to face Dominic.

"I wanted to know more about you," she said. "I wanted to find out about you."

He reached past her, shutting off his computer monitor with a soft click. "You saw me," he said flatly. "What I was."

She nodded.

"Feel cheated?" The bitterness in his voice was palpable, and she saw his fear and reticence, past the scars in his face.

She cupped his mauled cheek in her palm. "Absolutely not," she said. "I don't care about that."

He pulled away from her. "Then what the hell did you want to find out? It's all in the past. It's not important."

"I want to know everything about you," she whispered, following him as he tried to escape to the bedroom. "Who you were. Who you *are.*"

He sat on the bed, sending her an impassioned look. "You know me well enough."

"It's *not* enough," she protested.

"What if I told you that's all you're going to get?"

She let out a loud, frustrated sigh. "Don't treat me like a child!"

"I think you're forgetting the rules of this situation," he said sharply, standing up and stepping close to her. There was no pleading in his look now. He projected sternness . . . ferocity. "I *own* you. You do what I . . ."

"Shut up!" she said, shoving him. Or at least, trying to shove him. She put her hands on his chest but couldn't move him an inch. "If all I am is a slave to you, some little plaything, then go ahead. Punish me. Stop me from asking anything. Shut yourself off. But we both know that I care about you. And you care about me, if you'd just be honest with yourself."

He glared at her, bearing down on her, his expression full of menace.

She crossed her arms, glaring back.

"What the hell do you want to know?" he said finally.

Her mind rushed with questions. "Everything."

"I was born to a hooker in Alameda, California," he said, his voice a dull monotone. "I don't know who my father was. My Mom didn't give a shit about me. She kept me around for welfare money until she got a better pimp and I went into foster care. I joined a gang when I was fourteen. And then I did every bad thing imaginable. Is that what you wanted to know?"

His voice was deceptively casual, but each word lashed out like a whip. She swallowed hard, hearing the pain in every syllable.

"Because I was so good-looking, lots of women wanted to fuck me. I got a lot of attention. My nickname was Prettyboy. Because of a woman, I got a chance at getting into a big gang lord's house. He'd ordered a hit on a friend of mine. His wife wanted a piece of me, so I got into their house and I killed him. Is that what you wanted to know?"

She shook her head. "Dominic . . ."

He grabbed her arms, forcing her to look into his face. "Made myself a big name, then. Moved to Vegas. Traveled the world. Did whatever they asked me to. Had more money, more guns, more pussy thrown at me than I knew what to do with. Thought I'd finally joined a family, people who gave a shit about me. But when I wouldn't play ball, my ex-lover tries to take me out. Do you know how many people I had to kill to ensure my own safety? How many years I've had to fend for myself?"

He pushed her, pinned her to the bed, looming over her like a demon.

"Tell me, Nadia . . . *Is that what you wanted to know?*"

She ached to hold him, to somehow ease the searing agony she could sense coming off of him like heat from the Nevada desert. His eyes burned with a terrifying, scorching fury.

"I *knew* you'd keep pushing. Knew that you wouldn't be satisfied until you'd gotten to hear about my past," he said. "And you know what's even worse? I knew I'd tell you. You know *why?*"

She shook her head.

"Because I know you can't stay here," he said, and his voice broke. He let her go, rolling away from her. "It's stupid to keep you. You don't deserve this. You don't deserve *me.*"

He closed his eyes, turning away from her.

She tugged at him, urging him back. Holding him when he wouldn't budge. "Why do you say that?"

"I've done terrible things." His voice was a low monotone.

"So have I," she said.

"I've been an enforcer," he muttered. "A thief. Murderer."

"I've been a whore," she said. "I come from a family of thieves and prostitutes. It's not who I am now." She forced him to turn to her. "It's not who *you* are now."

He shook his head. "Don't try that. For Christ's sake, don't try to five-second psychoanalyze me."

"All right. You're an enforcer, thief and murderer," she said.

He nodded, finally turning to her, looking miserable.

She stroked his face. "I don't care."

"Bullshit."

She growled at him. Then she kissed him, gently first, then harder.

He shoved her away.

She felt tears sting at the corners of her eyes. Then pure, unadulterated anger sang through her bloodstream.

She tackled him.

She was gratified to see the look of surprise on his face—obviously, he didn't see this coming. She tried kissing him again. He struggled away from her. Finally, with a low roar, he spun, pinning her to the mattress again. "Enough!"

"No, it isn't," she hissed, and wrapped her legs around his waist, her arms around his neck, clinging to him like a barnacle.

He bucked against her—a familiar sensation. He was wearing clothes. She wasn't. His belt buckle chafed against her stomach, but she tightened her grip, kissing whatever she could reach.

"*Damn it.*" He finally got loose, breaking the grip of her arms. "Have you lost your mind?"

"Yes!" She grabbed for him, and he held her wrists, trapping her against the bed. They were both breathing heavily, staring at each other. "I'm not going to let you do this," she rasped.

"Do what?"

She raised an eyebrow. "Be all sacrificial and noble. You think you're not good enough for me. I don't care, and I'll prove it to you."

He stared at her, his mouth working even though words didn't come out. Finally, he frowned. "How do you plan on doing that?"

"By staying."

"For how long?"

She swallowed.

"Forever."

He went still. Then, with a low, tortured moan, he reached down, tearing open his fly, shoving his pants down past his hips. He nudged at her legs and she opened them eagerly. His massive cock strained against her stomach, and he shoved himself inside her, filling her with shocking speed. She cried out in gratitude as he slid into her body. She needed this. Needed *him*.

He surged up inside her, his body shifting and straining, his cock plunging inside her. It was rough, and quick, and harsh. His hips slammed against her, and she arched and screamed, forcing her hips against his, meeting him thrust for thrust. They were like animals, clawing at each other, their lips and teeth feasting wherever they could. He held her buttocks as he bucked, and she bit his shoulder as she screamed his name. She could feel the exquisite foretaste of climax shivering through her, and she moved mindlessly against him, her thighs tightening, her pussy clenching around his long, hard shaft.

"Nadia!" he roared, and as if triggered, her orgasm shattered her. She shrieked with the pleasure of it, and was gratified to feel his shuddering, pulsing release, hot and deep within her.

When it was over, he collapsed against her, his heavy breathing heating her neck. He held her tightly, as if afraid she would disappear.

She kissed his head, gently, cradling him against her.

She knew what she'd just agreed to. And, God help her . . . she meant every word.

Chapter Eight

Jelena wandered through the crowd, forcing herself to loosen her grip on her champagne flute before she shattered it.

The woman you're looking for is Alexis Carmello. You won't be able to miss her.

Jelena met April at her apartment, getting the contact information . . . and, she admitted, having sex with April one more time. It had been much more intimate and exciting without Phillipe there. April admitted she was more interested in women than men, although she had learned to enjoy herself plenty with either, especially under Phillipe's tutelage.

"Why are you involved with him anyway?" Jelena had asked her, as they lay naked in April's queen-sized bed.

April sighed. "I came from a rough background," she

whispered. "Everyone I knew used, or hooked, or . . . you know. I couldn't afford to go to college, couldn't get scholarships, had a record. I tried to rob Phillipe one night in sheer desperation. He offered to help me out."

"At what price?" Jelena asked, with horrified fascination.

April hadn't answered, but the look on her face was answer enough. It had been easy to have sex with her then, if only to try and distract her from the obvious pain she'd gone through.

It honestly hadn't been a hardship, she admitted. For one thing, April had toys, and she knew how to use them. Jelena hadn't come that much in her life. Her body still hummed with the thrall of it . . . no pun intended.

Jelena still couldn't quite understand or believe what had happened. First she'd seduced Robert, getting turned on by both the illicit aspect and the power. Now she was somehow getting involved with a younger woman, and having the best sex of her life. She was getting more depraved by the minute.

What's worse . . . she was beginning to enjoy it.

She'd never really thought of herself as a sexual being before. Well, that wasn't entirely true: obviously, if she weren't sexual, she wouldn't have been able to land Henry. But she was not someone who had thought overly of her own sexual needs. Now she was thinking about it, often. The idea of having sex with almost anyone didn't bother her, although she obviously didn't want it to be someone completely distasteful. But the fact that it might be temporary, or transactional, or whatever, no longer created any havoc in her sense of security.

Being desired, and acting on those desires, had added a certain lope to her step. She was less deer, more lioness. Being a huntress rather than prey—now that, she really enjoyed.

She unwittingly made eye contact with a man across the room. He responded with a sensual, predatory smile of his own.

She looked away, disinterested. She had only one target tonight.

Jelena frowned as she honed her focus. She was looking for a woman with jet-black hair, clear olive skin, and movie-star good looks. She'd probably be wearing black, white or red, her signature colors. The crowd was upscale; lots of women were wearing black.

You won't be able to miss Alexis. At least, that's what April said.

She was about to give up when suddenly a gap shifted in a knot of people, off in a corner by the bar. She saw the center of the group, the one who held them all in thrall and was acting as if she were holding court rather than attending a cocktail party.

Alexis.

The woman was tall, easily close to six feet. Her jet-black hair shone like polished onyx and was cut severely, not a strand out of place. Her face was porcelain-perfect, her icy gray eyes cutting. Her lipstick was a deep wine red. She looked like a vampire. She was wearing black clothes, as April had predicted, a black halter dress that looked vintage, yet showed off the woman's sensual curves so perfectly that it seemed bleeding-edge modern. Most of the people surrounding her were men, Jelena noticed. The woman's lazy smile seemed to take this into account, as well.

Jelena swallowed hard, feeling some of her newfound confidence start to ebb. Bad enough to approach a stranger at a cocktail party, something she hated under any circumstances. But this? Approach this Amazon, in the middle of all her admirers? How the hell was she supposed to do *that*?

As she was considering it, the woman answered the question for her. She broke away from her throng of admirers, ignoring or waving off the hands that tried to stop her. For a moment, Jelena was afraid she was too late, that the woman was already leaving the party. Instead, the woman disappeared down a hallway.

Jelena followed her, heart hammering in her chest.

Don't tell me you're stalking this woman to the bathroom. It was beyond humiliating.

Still, what choice did she have?

She waited until the woman reappeared in the hallway. She took in Jelena's hesitant form with a sort of sneer.

"Ms. Carmello?"

Alexis barely looked at her, obviously making a casual mental dismissal, and started to walk around her.

Jelena stepped in front of her, blocking her exit.

"What do you want?" Alexis drawled, her eyes showing her obvious irritation.

"I have information that you might find very interesting," she said, as April had prepped her. God, she felt like a reject from a bad spy film, though.

"I sincerely doubt that," Alexis responded. "Get out of my way."

"I really need your help . . ."

Alexis took a step closer, her face inches from Jelena's. "Move, or I'll move you."

She sounded too bored for it to be a real threat, but Jelena saw the promise of violence in the woman's gray eyes.

"I want revenge on Dominic Luder," Jelena whispered. "I need your help."

Alexis's eyes flashed with hatred, but her expression remained schooled, impassive. "Anyone could say that. How am I supposed to know you're on the level?"

This was what April warned her of. "Any test you want, I'll do it."

The black-haired woman's lips pursed. "Anything, hmm?"

Jelena nodded.

The woman stared at her, her gaze boring into Jelena. It was all Jelena could do to stop from squirming. Finally, the woman reached into her miniscule purse, producing a card.

"This is my place," she said. "Stop by, and we'll see what we can set up."

She walked away. Jelena stood still, making sure she wouldn't tremble from the adrenaline pumping through her system. When she was finally sure she had herself under control, she looked down at the card.

Earthly Delights.

This was the brothel. Alexis's brothel. There was an address, but no phone number.

There was also a little note, printed in a shiny foil.

V.I.P.

This was what she needed. Now, she just had to pass the test.

Nadia's not happy.

It had been a few days since she'd gone into his room; since he'd made his confession, and she'd made her promise. She'd stay forever, she said. He didn't believe her, but some absurd part of him really wanted to.

He hadn't left the house since. They'd spent a lot of time together, having sex obviously, but also talking—probably due to sheer exhaustion. Now that he'd opened up a bit, he felt almost helpless to stop himself from sharing more and more, about his past, his dreams, his disappointments. She'd listened carefully, without judgment. She hadn't given advice or any comment beyond support. She'd held him, somehow making the more painful memories ease. And she'd done the same. He now knew that her mother had died in an accident on a train track, and some people had speculated that it had been suicide. Her father had kept them together however he could, but staying on the straight and narrow never worked for him. She'd been desperately poor, hungry, and determined to survive.

He knew she was beautiful. Now, he thought she was unbelievable.

When they didn't talk, they ate, comparing their favorite foods and experimenting with new ones. He'd watched movies with her. Apparently, she hadn't watched a lot of cartoons, and he couldn't remember feeling as happy as he did hearing her laugh.

It felt dangerously like a relationship. He tried to return to sex whenever he could, to feel a bit calmer about the whole thing. Even that had changed, though. The dynamic had shifted. She slept in his bed now. She gave Max his nighttime treat, for Christ's sake.

He was in trouble.

She walked in front of him, nude except for a coquettish set of cherry-red heels that she knew he liked. Her hips swayed lyrically, and her hazel eyes heated him all the way through his core.

"Nadia," he growled.

She walked to him eagerly, reaching for him, unzipping his pants as he sat in the leather chair by the fireplace. It was one of his favorite places to take her, and she knew it. She spread the fly open, reaching in, freeing him from his boxers. His cock sprang out, tearing itself from its confinement. She stroked him, still with that knowing smile.

God, how I want this woman.

He tugged at her hips, and she parted her legs willingly, straddling him, impaling herself on his cock. She moaned softly as his cock pierced her, the thick head nuzzling her curls before parting her already damp folds. She was wet for him. Could you fake that kind of thing? No. She was *drenched* for him.

It still baffled him, humbled him. Made him want her all the more.

Her knees braced on either side of his thighs, she slowly raised herself up and down, the friction of her pussy massaging his penis making him shudder with longing.

"Dominic," she breathed, arching her back slightly. Her breasts pressed forward, rosy nipples offering themselves like Christmas presents. He didn't deny their appeal, instead leaning forward, sucking hard on first one, then the other. She gasped, slamming hard against him, ramming his cock upward inside her. Her body squeezed against him tightly.

"You feel so damned good," he growled against her hot skin, nuzzling her with the rough day's growth of beard along his jaw line. She pressed his face against her breasts, holding him tight as she wriggled her hips in that slow circular motion that made him crazy. He held her hips firmly against him, his cock tracing inside her in the way he knew she loved. As she always did, she started to rock against him, her breathing going slightly faster.

She wrapped her legs around his waist, forcing him to scoot out a bit, toward the edge of the chair. To his surprise, she moved his head back, forcing him to look at her. He winced, not wanting to see her looking at his face, but all he saw was the tenderness inherent in her gaze. Then she closed those doe-like eyes of hers, and her lips found his, unerringly. Her kiss was sweet, soft, hot. He started with surprise when her tongue traced his lips. Then, slowly, he opened his mouth, letting her tongue explore. The soft seeking motion was intoxicating, and soon his tongue was tangled with hers, stroking . . . tasting.

The feel of his tongue in her mouth as his cock was buried in her pussy was unbelievable. They writhed together, bound together, opening by opening. A light sheen of sweat covered her. He wanted to feel her, all of her. He broke away only for a moment to tear off his shirt, then he clenched her against him, her slick skin sliding against his as he pressed closer, closer.

She was starting to move more rapidly, less gracefully, the heat between them unbelievable. His hips flexed beneath her, his whole body taut with exertion as he surged inside of her.

"Ah . . . ah . . . oh, God, yes . . ." she murmured, adding things in Russian he didn't understand, but obviously were a product of the moment. Hearing her voice, rough with passion, the way her breathing was so ragged, sending a wave of heat through him. She was close. He held her tight, angling his cock, searching for her button.

She screamed, and he felt her pussy convulse around him as waves of wetness washed over his cock, his thighs. He smiled, holding on tight to what tenuous control he had over his own response.

When her breathing slowed, she kissed him again, languorous and tender. "Did you?"

He shook his head, and she smiled with delight. "How do you . . ."

He stood up, carrying her with him. He kicked off his pants, then stretched her out on the plush oriental carpet. She reached for him as he covered her with his body. He angled her legs up against his chest, allowing him to penetrate her that much more deeply.

Her breathing went shallow. He went slowly, carefully . . . withdrawing almost entirely, then slowly pressing in with his full length. Her ankles rested lightly on his chest. He saw her clit, resting there over the space where his shaft disappeared inside her. Slowly, deliberately, he stroked her with hard pressure from his thumb. After a few minutes, he saw her nipples go hard again, a slight flush on her skin. She was clawing at the rug, biting her lip, her hips swaying as he continued his relentless invasion.

He waited until she was moaning again before allowing himself to consider giving in to his own need. His tempo picked up, incrementally, his jutting thrusts moving in time with the pressure of his thumb.

She reached up, caressing her own breasts, kneading them as he watched. Heat boiled through him, lust spearing him like a lance. "Dom-Dominic," she stammered. "Dominic, I'm going to . . . again . . ."

He knew what she meant, and his cock throbbed painfully as it realized release might be near. He closed his eyes, plunging inside her, losing control. He felt the tremors of her orgasm, shuddering against him, and it was more than he could handle. He yelled in triumph as his own orgasm roared through him, almost painful in its intensity. She cried out in response, and he felt her clutch around his engorged pole, milking his climax, drawing it out.

When it was over, he collapsed momentarily against her before rolling, taking her with him, resting her against his heaving chest. He was still buried inside her, still feeling that delicious, unpredicted sense of closeness.

I love this woman.

He kissed the top of her head. "What shall we do today?" he rumbled, feeling at peace with the world. "Besides more of this, at any rate."

She smiled, but somehow, the smile didn't completely reach her eyes.

"What?" he finally asked, stroking her cheek. "What's wrong?"

She sighed, and he braced himself.

"I . . . miss my family."

His frown was fierce. *Why?* was his first thought. After all, her father was a two-bit loser who saw his daughters as a form of income. For God's sake, they'd abandoned her, left her to the mercy of . . .

His frown deepened. Well, they'd left her with *him*. Which spoke pretty damned poorly of their judgment.

She read his face, and shook her head. "I know," she murmured.

Abruptly, he felt a wave of remorse. She'd listened to his past without judging. And she, for whatever reason, seemed to care about him. He probably shouldn't throw stones.

God, he wanted to see her happy.

As she eased herself off of his lap, he cleared his throat. "Maybe you could call them."

He blinked. Good grief, had he just suggested that?

She perked up, and he cursed himself silently. "Call?"

"You know. Check in. Let them know you're all right." *Let them know you're staying with me for the rest of your life, so they can just find a meal ticket elsewhere. And about time, too.*

She brightened like the sun. He felt like an asshole for not suggesting it earlier. He offered her his phone. She pressed a quick, fervent kiss on his lips, and he suddenly felt like a king. She crossed the room, but didn't leave it. As he got himself pulled together, he heard the conversation. He probably shouldn't be eavesdropping, he realized—but it wasn't going to keep him up nights. He wasn't a fucking saint.

"Jelena!" she cried out happily. Her sister. She'd gotten through. "No, no, I'm fine, I'm all right."

His lips quirked at that one. *More than all right,* he thought, zipping his pants.

"Well . . . no. I'm still at Dominic Luder's house." There was a long pause, and she shot him a cautious look. Her voice lowered. "Jelena, it's not like that. He hasn't hurt me."

Ouch.

Nadia's beautiful features frowned. "I would not say forced," she said awkwardly, shooting another look at him.

The sister was asking about sex. Asking if he'd raped her. He rubbed his hands over his face.

Why did I think this was a good idea, again?

"He gave me his cell phone, Jelena," Nadia said, with obvious irritation. "No, I'm not a prisoner . . ."

Abruptly, she shifted to rapid, fluid Russian. He couldn't figure out exactly what she was saying, but he could see her happiness disappear, replaced with a tension that tightened her shoulders, making her hunch with displeasure. Finally, Nadia barked out something to stop her sister's quick, sharp-toned remarks. She sighed.

"I love you, my sister," she said. "I will see you when I can."

With that, she hung up, handing the phone back to him. Her eyes looked more haunted.

"That went well," he said sarcastically. "What's her problem?"

"Just a family thing." Her words were taut as piano wire. "At least the baby seems to be doing okay."

"Your stepmother's baby?" he asked. "Your . . . what, half brother, right?"

She nodded. Then she paused, and he knew, just *knew*, that something was coming.

"She's having a C-section on the twenty-eighth," Nadia said softly. "I'd like to go. To see it."

At first, his brain didn't process the request. Then, anger and fear pummeled him, a one-two punch.

She's asking to leave.

"So much for forever," he grunted, starting to turn away.

She put a hand on his shoulder. "I wouldn't be gone long . . ."

"I don't want to hear it." He was probably being childish. *You know what? Fuck it. Getting blown up by the woman you thought you loved probably gave you some leeway as far as immaturity.* "You said you didn't want to leave. Well, I don't feel like letting you go."

"They're my *family*."

"They haven't cared about you!" he spat out. "What the hell sort of loyalty do you owe them? I only let you call because I thought it would make you happy, and *now* look at you!"

That seemed to slap at her. She froze. Then, slowly, a tear crawled down her cheek.

"Damn it." He let out a sharp hiss of breath. "Don't do that. Don't blackmail me with tears. It just won't work."

He fled, feeling like even more of an ass, but unsure of how to make the transition. He cared about her. She'd go, and once she was outside the little cocoon of intimacy they'd created, things would get messed up—he knew that for a fact. She'd leave, and then things would go to hell in a hurry. Her family would need her. They'd convince her he was a monster. They'd finally and irrefutably prove that her promise was just the result of her captivity, a complete lack of perspective.

He knew this, because it gnawed at him daily.

He shut himself in his room. Yes, it was childish. But right now, it was the best that he had . . . because the alternative was losing Nadia for good, and he wasn't strong enough for that.

Chapter Nine

Why won't he trust me?

Nadia had never been in this situation before. She wasn't sure how or when things got so absolutely complicated, but she was going to find a middle ground or die trying.

Sex seemed to be the only common ground that they had, lately. She didn't mind that, in a lot of ways. She loved the feel of his powerful body when it moved inside her, the way every touch brought out a myriad of sensations and feelings. She *craved* him. She wanted him with every fiber of her being. But at the same time, she felt so much because he allowed her to be herself. She didn't have to pretend anymore. She'd never felt so authentic, certainly not with her own family. She'd been focused on survival for so long, she didn't realize that she could feel anything more.

Now, though, she had gotten greedy. She wanted more than simply tepid statements that they cared for each other. She wanted him to trust her. She wanted more with him than a sequestered fantasy existence, where they hid from his death threats and her family. They had a relationship, damn it. They could make it work in real life, if he weren't being such a . . . what was the American word that best fit?

Butthead. If he weren't being such a butthead.

Still, things weren't so straightforward that she could simply yell at him that he was being a butthead, slap some sense into him—metaphorically speaking—and then expect him to understand. He'd developed his beastlike tendencies under torture, abandonment, and abuse.

Tough love was not what was needed here, though she wasn't quite sure what the alternative was.

He hid himself in his lair, sulking. She waited until ten o'clock that night. She even pulled together some dinner, which he never touched. By ten, she realized that he was simply going to avoid her as long as possible, until she caved. Well, that wasn't going to work.

She banged on the door to his bedroom suite with her fist. "Dominic? Dominic! You can't keep hiding from me!"

He opened the door, his eyes gleaming like onyx in the dim light. "I'm not hiding." The words were brittle.

"I'm not going anywhere," she said, crossing her arms in front of her. "Not until we talk about this."

"What is it with women, always wanting to talk? Talk isn't going to get us anywhere. You've got your choices. You stay, or you go. That's it."

That glower of his used to terrify her. Now, she knew he was simply buckling up all his armor. Protecting himself.

A frontal assault was not going to work, she realized, her heart sinking. It was just as well—she only had so much energy to fight. No, if this were going to happen, then she was going to just have to find another way past his defenses.

He would listen to her. She just needed to find a different way to communicate.

She took a deep breath. "Fine. I won't talk about . . . that."

He shrugged. "Fine." He started to close the door again.

"So that's it? You're not going to even . . ." She made a vague gesture with her hands. "Be . . . with me?"

"Excuse me for not being in the mood for sex right now." His words were tinged with frost.

What did he expect her to do? Beg? She'd be damned before she . . .

She took a deep breath. Sighed. Gritted her teeth. "Please?"

His eyes widened, and his scarred face twisted sarcastically. "I see. Well, that certainly makes a difference."

"Give me at least the chance to change your mind," she said, her voice soft, an almost whisper. All right, she was begging. *In a good cause,* she thought.

He sighed, then opened the door. Cautious, she stepped inside. He didn't want to be pitied. He didn't want to be vulnerable. This was where he felt safest. This was where he went to lick his wounds.

I'll just have to lick his wounds for him.

The thought was a soothing balm. She'd approached him the wrong way. She still needed his trust as well as his love, but he was scared. He didn't want to lose her, but he couldn't believe that she really wanted to stay. Couldn't conceive that she actually accepted him, flaws and all. She had to show him that.

She smiled softly.

"What?" he asked, his voice thick with suspicion. "What are you thinking?"

"You've got a big bed," she said speculatively. He had a fireplace as well.

"I mean it," he said, his tone stern. "I'm not in the mood."

She realized that. She sat on the edge of his bed. "Then can I ask you a few questions?"

He glanced at her suspiciously. "About what?"

"About the fetish stuff," she said. "When I first got here, you had 'punishments' for me. It was different—more like a game. I'd never done anything like that before."

He sighed, deeply. "I shouldn't have," he said. "Once we . . . well, once things changed between us, I made sure to stop."

Her mouth fell open. "Wait, *no*. I'm not bringing that up to make you feel badly. I didn't mean that at all!"

"So you're not trying to guilt me into letting you go?"

"Absolutely not." She felt appalled. This was worse than she thought. "I was just going to ask: have you always enjoyed that sort of thing?"

He was silent, standing still. She could feel the tension of him, the discomfort.

Shame.

She walked over to where he was, and he flinched, as if he would take a step back. "You didn't hurt me," she said.

His snort of disbelief was punctuated by his cold blue stare.

"Really." She took his hand, stroking it, feeling the muscles bunch and flex beneath her palm. "I was surprised by it. I enjoyed parts of it." Her eyes dropped to the ground. "I didn't think I should."

She felt his fingers below her chin, urging her face up to meet his gaze. "Are you just saying this, Nadia?"

She shook her head, realizing she wasn't. "I am curious. How did you know that those things could be . . . ?"

"Pain—a small, controlled amount—can blur into pleasure." His voice was low, so low she had to strain to hear it. "But you didn't know that. I didn't even establish boundaries with you. Trust me, I of all people should have known better."

"Who taught you?" The question popped out unbidden, and she bit her lip once it was aloud.

He closed his eyes. "Alexis."

Jealousy stabbed at her. Of course, Alexis. She stroked his arm. "I didn't mean to remind you of those times."

"No. I just . . . hadn't thought of it in a long time." He seemed to calm under her stroking, although he still didn't look at her. "You saw what I used to look like."

She paused a moment, then continued to stroke him, hoping to ease him through what he was remembering.

"My mom used to say I was useless except for my looks," he said. "When I got old enough for women to notice it, my face got me anything I wanted. It made men hate me. I got my ass kicked a lot. Then I got tough, and that stopped." He said that with brutal relish. "I had whatever woman I wanted. It got to be almost too easy. Then I met Alexis."

He said her name like his tongue was sliding over a razor. Nadia shivered.

"She taught me that pain and pleasure could be close. She taught me how to punish . . ." He stopped abruptly, looking at Nadia warily.

"Go on," she urged quietly.

He took a deep breath. "I knew what her limits were. How to make her feel just enough pain; when to stop. She taught me how to play the game. Sometimes I thought I loved her, and sometimes I thought I hated her. But I never forgot her, and I've never felt anything quite like it."

He stopped, looking at Nadia with awkward embarrassment.

"After the bomb, why didn't you just . . ." She stopped, realizing what she was about to propose.

"Kill Alexis?" he asked, reading her mind. "I have thought about it. But I couldn't."

"Why not?"

"Because I've never felt anything like the way she made me feel, good and bad," he said. Then he grimaced. "I'm sorry. I didn't mean to tell you all that."

"I know." And she loved him more for it—for the fact he felt like he could tell her anything. "Do you miss it?"

"Miss what?" Then he paused, realizing what she meant. "Do I miss those . . . games?"

She nodded.

"I wouldn't ask that of you, Nadia," he said, his voice gravelly. "You're better than that."

"It's not a matter of better or not. It's just what feels good, and what doesn't. I want you to show me," she whispered. "I trust you."

He looked pensive for a moment. Then he took her to the bed. "Lie down."

She did, and he took out what looked like several black silk scarves. "If there's *anything* you don't want to do . . ."

"I'll tell you," she said immediately.

He still hesitated. Then, slowly, he rolled her onto her stomach, stretching her arms behind her and binding her wrists. She felt a jolt of apprehension, her heart beating rapidly. He bound her ankles as well; snug enough to know she couldn't move, although not enough to be painful. She twisted her body to look at him.

"Are you all right?" he asked instantly.

She nodded, unable to speak. He looked strained. Then, he took the last silk scarf, and covered her eyes, plunging her into darkness.

She felt unbelievably vulnerable. Every sense except for sight was heightened. She could smell the woodsy aroma of the fire, mixed with slight tinge of expensive cologne that he wore. She could feel the softness of the sheets below her sliding across her skin. Her nipples dragged as she rolled slightly.

She could feel the warmth of his palms dancing millimeters away from her skin, not actually touching her, and the hair at the nape of her neck prickled with awareness. Then she felt his breath against her shoulder, her neck.

He rolled her onto her back, the awkwardness of her binding making her chest jut forward. She felt his breath between her breasts, teasing them, taunting them.

Then she felt his broad palm on her throat, his fingers gently curving around her neck.

She couldn't help it: she gasped, her body tensing at the exact moment he took her nipple into his mouth. The juxtaposition of feelings—fear, pleasure—was like an electric shock. She gasped louder as he began to suckle, drawing her deep into his mouth, the pulsing pull of pressure sending waves of delight over her skin. She writhed beneath him, and his hand tightened ever so slightly around her throat. She could still breathe easily. He switched breasts, increasing his ministrations. She rubbed her thighs together, suddenly slick with the wetness of her growing arousal.

He removed his hand from her neck, smoothing it down her body . . . lower, until he spread her thighs as much as her bound ankles would allow. His fingers teased their way between her damp folds, stroking and stretching. He moved his head lower, pressing hot kisses down her solar plexus, her stomach, toward the area where his fingers were moving so industriously. He found her clit with his hands, and manipulated it deftly, waves of sensation pulsing up from between her legs. Her heart beat like a trip-hammer, and she moaned softly, lifting her hips as best she could off the bed, enticing him.

He nipped her hip, hard. She gasped. It hurt, a little—but

again, he'd timed it so it was just as her body was starting to wriggle with precursors of orgasm. It was as if the pain only pitched the fevered feelings of ecstasy higher.

She had no idea how long he kept this up—it seemed interminable, as if she were burning in a flame of desire that would not find release. She had never felt this hot before. Every time her breathing sped up, every time she got to the delicious edge of orgasm, he would pull back, adjust her position, give her time to cool down as he kissed her or massaged her breasts, her hips, her legs.

Finally, he turned her over, onto her knees, her hips up in the air. She shivered, knowing he was going to finally enter her. He plunged his fingers inside her, giving her a foretaste of the penetration she really wanted.

"Dominic," she breathed, "please . . ."

She felt the spank, short and sharp, across her right buttock.

She squealed in surprise as her ass felt a burst of heat and pain. Did she want this? She didn't want . . .

The next strike was exactly the same . . . except she felt the tip of his cock, thick and hard, pressing into her.

Suddenly, the dynamic changed. The pain of each spank was counterpointed by the smooth, sensual glide of his cock, moving inch by inch inside her. She found herself lolling her head from one side to another, backing her hips to meet each thrust, each soft blow from the palm of his hand. She shivered as the emotions blurred to a chaotic frenzy of high-pitched desire.

"Dominic!" she screamed, as he started to thrust harder,

his deep penetration and hard, slamming thrusts replacing his palm. "Dominic! *Dominic!*"

He groaned loud, his pace frenzied as her bucking motions against him. He covered her, reaching around to cup her breasts, his hips jerking against hers. The feel of his chest against her back, the heat of his hips against her buttocks, the kneading pressure of her breasts, the wonderful feel of his hard, thick cock inside her . . . it was finally too much. The orgasm exploded through her like a grenade, and she shrieked in pure animal pleasure. His loud groan of pleasure as he shuddered inside her blended with hers, and his hips jerked hard against her as he spilled himself into her.

They fell to their sides, spooning, sweaty and breathing hard. She felt dazed. Her whole body throbbed.

He kissed her hair, her shoulder. She could feel the tension that replaced the bliss of their lovemaking. He undid her wrists and ankles, saving her blindfold for last. When she could see again, she saw the regret and pain in his face.

She reached up, cupping his jaw, then kissed him, tenderly and deeply.

"I didn't hurt you?"

"I've never felt anything like it," she said. "And we can do it again whenever you like."

He crushed her to him, holding her tight with evident relief.

She curved around him, snuggling against him. "I won't leave you," she murmured. "I won't ever desert you. I wouldn't hurt you, I won't betray you."

"Shhh," he murmured, stroking her hair. "Don't."

"You have to believe me," she said fiercely. "Please."

He shuddered. "Don't," he repeated, and the word seemed torn from him.

She propped herself up on one elbow. "I want you to trust me," she breathed. "What would it take? To get you to trust me?"

"You're still trying to leave," he said, but the heat was gone.

"Just to see my family."

"What have those people done for you anyway?" His eyes were sharp, accusatory. "Your father sold you and your sisters like whores. You're not even related to your stepmother. Why should you have anything to do with them at all?"

She sighed. "I can't get you to understand," she said. "They've all done unpleasant things, for the good of the family. I don't agree with all of it now. But all of that lead me here, to you. Please, don't begrudge them doing what they thought was best."

"You're blind," he said. "You're hopelessly naïve. You're . . . dependent."

She shrugged. "I am who I am," she murmured. "I won't change that. Please don't ask me to."

His arms tightened around her. "I can't change, either."

"So there's no way you'll trust me," she said, and the truth of it, the weight of it, threatened to crush her.

He took a deep breath. "You won't want to betray me, maybe," he said grudgingly. "But . . ."

"I will come back to you," she breathed. "*I swear*, I will always come back to you."

He crushed her against him, kissing her with a passion that took her breath away.

"An hour," he croaked, when he finally pulled away. "An hour."

She sighed. "It would take longer than that to get to the city, and you know it. Besides, I want to spend at least a little time with the baby."

"How long do you think you'll need?"

She bit her lip. How long could he take being away from her?

For that matter, how long did she want to be away?

"One day," she said. "Maybe let me stay the night."

His face looked anguished. His eyes seemed to try to bore right through to her soul.

"One day," he finally agreed.

She felt exultant. Not because she was leaving him, but because he *trusted* her.

"But if you're not back in one day," he said, his words edged in menace. "I don't know what'll happen."

Was it supposed to be a threat to her? Or a threat to himself? She didn't know. All she knew was, he looked like he was watching his soul fly away, with a mixture of love and terror.

"Nadya! Darling!"

Nadia's father was quickly shushed by her sisters and her stepmother. In her stepmother's arms was the baby, a squashed, ruddy-faced miracle.

"Isn't he beautiful?" her stepmother cooed, not even looking at Nadia. "Isn't he precious?"

Nadia's father was beaming; he could barely contain himself. *Finally,* Nadia thought, *he's gotten the son he always wanted.* Three wives, four children, and he finally struck gold.

She stepped closer. The baby had the sort of wrinkled-peanut face that all newborns did, but Deidre was right: he *was* miraculous. Her heart clenched, looking at him.

"How did you escape?" her father asked, checking her over, and for a second, Nadia felt a flood of warmth at his concern. Until her father paled, glancing over her shoulder. "Are you sure you weren't followed? Would he track you *here*?"

She swallowed hard as tears choked her. "No, Papa, it's fine," she reassured him. "He let me leave."

The entire family stared at her in stunned silence.

"Just like that?" her father finally said. "He just . . . let you go? He's done with you?"

Nadia felt her cheeks heat with a blush. "No," she whispered. "I have to go back. But he knows this is important to me, so . . ."

"I don't understand," Irina said. "What, did he give you money for a taxi to the hospital or something?"

"Actually, he . . . ah, he loaned me a car."

Her father's eyes rounded. Then he burst out laughing, a loud, roaring sound that caused the baby to wriggle and start to cry. Deidre tried to shush both father and baby, frowning.

"I thought no one could tame the beast, but apparently I did not give my daughter enough credit," he said, his voice crowing with satisfaction. "You have saved us all, Nadia, pet. You are a miracle worker."

Irina sighed. "Yeah, but will it get us money?"

Her father's bright eyes turned speculative.

Nadia felt tears pricking at her eyelids, her chest squeezing. She should have known: saving their lives wouldn't quite be enough. She stroked the baby's smooth, amazingly soft cheek. He moved blindly toward her, settling down in his mother's arms, then yawned, the adorable baby-yawn.

"Come on, he's sleepy," Jelena said, getting up and making ushering motions toward her sisters. Nadia wasn't sure if it was to give their father some privacy with his new family, or what. Irina followed without a pause—babies really weren't her idea of entertainment. The three of them went to the lobby on the first floor of the hospital.

There was something different about Jelena, Nadia noticed, although she couldn't quite put her finger on what had changed. Her clothes were elegant, a skirt with a blouse, but her neckline was perhaps a little lower than normal. Her hair wasn't up in its usual twist, either. Nadia would almost say Jelena looked a little sensual, although it would be a hard argument seeing her next to Irina, who was hard at work husband-hunting in a tight, short ensemble that played up her twenty-four-year-old body to its best advantage.

In contrast to Jelena's subtle sensuality, there was Jelena's face. Her expression was like frozen marble, and there was a sternness there that Nadia had never seen before.

"How long have you been here?" Nadia asked carefully. "You look exhausted."

"A few hours. The C-section went perfectly." Jelena shrugged. So if it wasn't being at the hospital, then something else was causing that strained expression on her sister's face. "Are you all right?"

Nadia blinked. "Well, yes. Why wouldn't I be?"

"You're with *that man*." Jelena's eyes narrowed. "We thought he'd hurt you. Possibly even worse."

"Must have been hard, not knowing for sure," Nadia said, biting her lip. Her eyes misted.

Jelena sighed. "I have been trying to do whatever I could, to free you. To help you." Her voice broke on those last words, and that frozen expression on her face turned even more coldly determined. "You have no idea."

Before Nadia could pursue it, Irina interrupted. "She's divorcing Henry. Divorcing *him*," Irina said with heavy emphasis.

That might explain the stress. "I'm so sorry, Jelena . . ."

"I'm not." Jelena's voice was crisp. Her blue eyes were like blowtorches. "It's not important. You said you have to go back to him. What happens if you don't?"

"Jelena, are you nuts?" Irina said quickly in Russian. "He'll come after us!"

"So we should just sacrifice Nadia for our own safety?" Jelena's drawl was low and surprisingly sinister. "What happens when it's your turn to pitch in, Irina? Will you mind when we leave you to die?"

Nadia and Irina gaped. Jelena was usually so pragmatic, the

first to say that a woman's place was supporting her family. This change of attitude . . . "Jelena, are *you* all right?"

"How can you ask me that?" Jelena's laugh was rough, painful. "You're the one who's forced to stay with that . . . that *murderer*. That beast."

"You don't know him," Nadia said quickly.

Jelena's eyes widened. "Good God. And he's even got you defending him." Jelena looked pale. "I need to go outside."

Nadia watched as her eldest sister walked away unsteadily. "How long has she been like this?" she asked Irina softly.

Irina shrugged. "She's had a bug up her ass since you left," she said. "I figured her husband was cheating on her. They all do. Bastards."

"Has she moved in with the family, too, then?" Nadia asked. "With the divorce happening and all?"

"No, and here's the thing." Irina leaned forward, her eyes brightening as her voice lowered. "She's keeping the house. And I think she's getting a boatload of money, too. Despite the prenuptial agreement, can you believe it?"

Nadia gaped. Actually, she couldn't. Jelena was hardly a barracuda. She was more like a minnow . . . or at least, she had been. "Did father do something?"

"What could he do for her that he couldn't do for me?" Irina scoffed. "Besides, he's pissed at her, because she won't tell him how much money she has, and she's not giving him anything more than the usual stipend. *Man*, he was furious."

"I can imagine," Nadia murmured.

"He tried yelling at her. I thought he was even going to hit her," Irina confided. "But you know what she did? She just stood there, like an Amazon, and lifted her chin up. And she looked scary as hell."

Nadia could imagine that, too.

"So, do you think *The Beast* will agree to something?" Irina said. "You know, paying the family. We're really hurting since my divorce, and with the baby here, it's going to be tighter than ever. I can't spend *anything*."

Nadia grimaced. "I don't think so."

"Why not?" Irina asked, pouting. "That sucks. If he can afford a Testa Rossa, you *know* he's got lots of money. And you're sleeping with him, right? He likes you enough to let you borrow one of his cars. That sort of makes you, what, like a girlfriend? You should be able to squeeze some money out of him. Let him know it's important."

The avarice in Irina's voice turned Nadia's stomach. "Irina," Nadia murmured. "Did you worry about me at all?"

"Worry? Why?" Irina shrugged. "You're fine, right? I knew you would be."

"How did you know?" Nadia pressed.

"Bad things don't happen to you." Irina sighed. "After all, *you* didn't get married when you were eighteen, like the rest of us did. You haven't been divorced, and—"

"I'm going to go check on Jelena." She cut off Irina's irritated whine by getting up and stalking out the doors.

She found Jelena standing a ways off from the hospital doors, smoking a cigarette in a hand that trembled slightly. "I haven't seen you smoke since we were teens," Nadia said, walking up to her.

Jelena shrugged. "I've picked up all sorts of bad habits."

That sentence held a wealth of pain. Nadia scraped her toe on the sidewalk. "I'm sorry," she murmured. "About the divorce."

"There's no need for you to be sorry," Jelena said sharply. "I'm sorry I wasted so many years of my life trying to be perfect for him, trying to make him happy. So many years putting up with his *bullshit*."

Nadia recoiled from the venom in Jelena's voice, but her sister did not seem to notice.

"Sorry that I let him say all the things he did, basically calling me a whore for the arranged marriage. Making me feel like I owed him for every mouthful of food or piece of clothing I wore. And you know what I'm the most sorry about?"

Nadia shook her head, feeling a little scared.

"The fact that I did it all for our father, who can't keep his dick in his pants to save his life."

Nadia wouldn't have been more shocked if Jelena had punched her in the stomach.

"Why are we doing this, Nadia?" Jelena's eyes were glossy with unshed tears, and she put the cigarette out on the concrete with a harsh twist of her foot. "Our father, who has been bartering us away for his comfort since we were teens. The man who would rather steal cars than get a decent, boring job. Why do we keep hurting ourselves to help him?"

Nadia let out a low, quavering breath. She'd felt that way, but she'd kept all the resentments bottled up for so long . . . hearing them on her sister's lips was a revelation, slicing her open. Tears spilled down her cheeks.

Jelena saw them, and nodded. She took Nadia's hands.

"We don't have to," she said. "Not anymore. Come with me. I think I've figured out a way to protect you."

"No," Nadia said.

"Father doesn't deserve our help." Jelena looked grim. "I won't let the baby starve, or Deidre, they're innocent enough. But father is going to learn to live his own damned life."

"You're right about that," Nadia said. "But about me . . . I don't need protection from Dominic."

"Right," Jelena said with a sneer. "But you have to rush back to him. Because you *want* to, not because he's got you scared of what will happen if you don't go back."

"Yes," Nadia said quietly, realizing it was absolutely true.

Jelena studied Nadia's face carefully, then a look of dawning horror crept into her features. "You think you're in love with him, don't you?"

Nadia bit her lip, then lifted her chin slightly.

"He's broken you." Jelena's eyes lit with fury. "Twisted you."

"He's been broken," Nadia countered. "He is different."

"So, *what*—you're going to stay with him? Hope that he'll change . . . that he'll learn to be your lover instead of your keeper? That maybe you'll have some happy life with a man who is *keeping you prisoner*?"

"I know what it sounds like," Nadia said. "And if I tell you it's not that way, you won't believe me. I wouldn't believe me, either. But it really is different."

They stood there, silent, the words like a brick wall between them.

Finally, Nadia broke the silence. "I have to go," she said.

"It's a long drive. Give Papa and Deidre and the baby my love. I'll visit as soon as I can."

Jelena shuddered. "Go back to him, then. You don't know any better," her sister said dismissively.

"I'll be all right, Jelena," Nadia whispered, reaching for her sister's arm. Jelena tugged away. "Take care of yourself. You seem . . ." *Stressed? Damaged? Enraged? Insane?* Nadia couldn't come up with the right word, so she let the sentence trail off.

"You will be all right," Jelena muttered. "You'll see."

It sounded ominous.

Chapter Ten

Jelena sat in the lobby of Alexis's bordello with grim determination. She was going to have sex—not all that big a deal since by this time, sex had lost its risqué novelty. Now, however, she was going to pay for it. Honestly, she didn't want the sex. She was paying for a different service altogether: revenge against the man who had turned her sister into a complaisant, even willing, slave.

If it came with fucking, so be it.

A well-dressed, prim-looking young woman, wearing a severe black suit, her hair in a glossy French twist, walked up to where she was sitting. "Do you have an appointment?" she asked, not impolitely. More like a receptionist, all cool smiles and bored friendliness.

Jelena pulled Alexis's card out of her purse, and handed it to the woman. "I was invited."

The woman's eyes widened fractionally. "I'll have to see what we have available," she said, with a nod. "In the meantime, can I get you anything? Wine?"

"Do you have any vodka?"

"Of course. Gray Goose all right?"

Jelena took a deep breath. "If you've anything Russian . . ."

"Of course," the woman repeated warmly. "I'll be right back."

The woman went back to her ebony desk, quickly picking up the phone. Her voice was too low for Jelena to hear, but from the quick movements of her lips and the tightness of her expression, she got the feeling that Alexis's card was something special.

She only imagined what that meant, in the context of this place. Were the men extra well-hung or something? Talented?

What the hell am I going to have to prove now?

The receptionist had disappeared. When she returned to the lobby, she had a small selection of shot glasses, sitting like an arrangement of flowers in a bowl of crushed ice. "These are our best Russian vodkas," she offered, putting the bowl on an occasional table by Jelena's chair. "We'll have your room ready momentarily."

"No rush," Jelena found herself murmuring. She sampled two of the glasses. It was obviously expensive, going down smooth as silk before blooming fire in her chest, warming her throat. Her nerves calmed fractionally.

Until the receptionist returned. "They're ready for you now."

They are? What "they" was she referring to?

Jelena got up, following the girl down a maze of hallways. It was completely, almost eerily silent.

Soundproofing. Her heart started to pound.

The woman finally opened a door, ushering Jelena in. Alexis was sitting there, looking impeccable in a blood red dress with matching heels. She surveyed Jelena with amusement.

"You're not police," Alexis said. "I checked."

Jelena nodded. "I want . . ."

"Not so hasty." Alexis's voice was twice as smooth as the vodka. "You might not be on their payroll, but there's nothing to say that you wouldn't be working for them, nonetheless."

"If you knew anything about my family," Jelena said sharply, "you'd know helping the *politzya* is the last thing on my mind."

"Easy to say." Alexis stood. "You've come here. I imagine you'd like to sample the services."

Jelena shrugged. "Not particularly, but if that will convince you, then by all means."

Alexis's smirk was cold. "You're willing to fuck to get what you want. That's easy enough."

Jelena shrugged again, nerves causing her stomach to bunch. "And then we can discuss the real business at hand?"

"So professional." Alexis's tone was openly mocking. "I want to see how serious you are."

She opened a door. In walked one of the most handsome men Jelena had ever seen . . . totally nude.

She gasped in surprise. He was gorgeous—all of him. Chiseled muscles, gleaming with some kind of massage oil. Other than the abundant gold locks on his head, he was completely bare. *Completely.*

Strange, that of all the things involved in this scenario, *that* was what made her blush.

But the door didn't shut behind him. Instead, another man walked in. Equally gorgeous, only this time more exotic-looking. Asian, she wanted to say, perhaps mixed with Hispanic? His eyes were almond-shaped, his coloring a deep, burnished bronze. He was as tall as the blonde.

She felt her mouth go dry.

"Both?"

Alexis nodded.

"Concurrent," Jelena said, her voice cracking slightly, "or consecutive?"

Alexis burst out laughing. "As you like." She went through the door, her hand on the doorknob. "I'll give you an hour with my boys. Let them give you a good time. Then we'll discuss business."

The door shut quietly behind her.

Jelena studied the nude men. *Good lord.* She had no idea how to proceed on this.

"What are your names?" she asked slowly.

"Tom," the blonde said.

"Blade," the exotic one said. She noticed the blonde rolled his eyes, ever so slightly.

"Tom, Blade," she repeated, shaking her head. "Okay. What does she want me to do with you?"

"Whatever you want," Blade said, and the blonde nodded in agreement.

She stepped close to them, dropping her voice to a whisper. "I need her help," she said, low, fierce. "What will impress her?"

Tom's eyes narrowed. Then he looked at Blade, who shrugged.

"Maybe some music," Tom said. Blade went to a Bose stereo system, on the nightstand by the king-sized bed that now seemed to dominate the room. Music, something instrumental and jazz-fusion inspired, poured out.

To her surprise, Tom moved forward, wrapping her in his arms, pressing kisses on her face, then on her neck. He nibbled at her jaw line, her earlobe.

It felt marvelous.

"She's listening," he whispered in her ear. "Watching. You're being videotaped."

Jelena stiffened, and he covered her motion by biting her ear, causing her to gasp more audibly, her head tilting back.

"Don't let on," he whispered. Over his shoulder, she could see Blade, pulling back the bedsheets with a businesslike briskness. "If you want her help, she wants something she can blackmail you with. This is her insurance."

Jelena gritted her teeth. Of course. But what difference would a sex tape make? She wasn't running for office. She was trying to save her sister from a fate worse than death.

Worse. She was trying to save her sister from herself.

"All right," Jelena said, trying not to notice how good his hand felt as it cupped her ass, massaging her. He reached for the zipper on her skirt, undoing it, letting the garment drop to the floor. "Anything else?"

He looked into her eyes, kissing her deeply. He was an amazing kisser, she couldn't help but notice. Her nipples hardened despite herself.

"She believes that sex is power," he whispered, burying his face in her hair.

"Lot of that going around," Jelena muttered back, thinking of Phillipe.

"If you put on a good show . . . if you act like you believe the same thing . . ." He undid the buttons of her blouse. "Then she'll respect you."

Jelena shivered as he nibbled her neck. "All right."

She nudged him away, unbuttoning her blouse and tossing it aside. She removed her bra and panties and heels, and went to the bed. Blade was already stretched out, looking bored, she noticed. It was rude, really. What if she were a customer?

He wasn't hard, either: another sign of disrespect. She shoved him back onto the pillows. He looked a little surprised.

She kissed him as she grabbed his cock, brushing her rock-hard nipples against his bare chest. The feel of his shaven balls was strange, like rough silk under her fingertips. He groaned against her lips.

She felt Tom move behind her, his cock already stiffening, pressing against her buttocks as he spooned behind her, pressing hot, insistent kisses on her back. He seemed to know every strange, insistent erogenous zone she possessed. Without thinking, she stroked Blade's now-perky erection with more insistence, rubbing her thigh against his, feeling Tom's leg stretching behind hers.

Blade's breathing had sped up slightly, and he was kissing her back, his tongue invading her mouth. She grunted with irritation, shoving his face away. "Not like that," she said sharply, and he scowled at her. "You're here for *my* pleasure. You serve *me*."

She turned her back to him, reaching for Tom, kissing him. Tom's lips were warm, firm, pliant. He kissed her with gentle insistence, and the heat of nerves in her stomach turned into a different type of heat altogether. Sighing, she curved against him, his leg parting her thighs.

Blade growled with irritation. She didn't turn from Tom's face. "Blade," she said, against Tom's lips, "you're not pleasing me."

"But I will." His voice, low and rough, actually made her shiver. Then she felt him, kissing her back much as Tom had. Then she felt his hand cupping her bottom, his fingers delving gently for her cleft.

She let out a rough exhalation when he found what he was looking for. With more care than she would have given him credit for, he parted the folds of her, caressing the delicate inner flesh. She took a deep, shuddering breath as Tom moved from her face to her breasts, kissing first one, then the other . . . then suckling one gently as his hand traced the opposite nipple with a delicate, experienced hand. She arched her back slightly, pressing her breasts deeper into his wet, hot mouth. Blade spread her legs, and she felt the prickle of his short haircut between her thighs, the blaze of his breath against her quickly dampening flesh.

When he suckled on her clit, she moaned loudly, closing her eyes. The sensation was unbelievable, more than she ever would have imagined. Her hips gyrated against his insistent, mobile tongue. He laved her, his tongue tracing her every line, every hidden crease. Jets of heat shot through her, from her breasts, from her pussy.

"Yes," she said, mindful of her audience. *"Yes."*

She spread her legs a bit further, and Blade edged upward, his chin moving, making way for . . . she felt a broad finger trace the opening of her pussy, then delve deep, as his teeth grazed her now rock-hard clit. She cried out at the sensation, and he nibbled, making it increase ten-fold. It was almost too much.

His finger stroked carefully, in and out, as if he were simply taking her measure. Then, after some searching, he finally found the sensitive spot, high and inside. She growled, letting him know what he'd discovered. Tom laughed, nipping at her throat.

"Suck on me," she said, not sure which man she was ordering. "Hard."

Both did as requested. Tom kissed her throat, his mouth drawing enough pressure to cause pain, surely enough to leave a mark. It was eclipsed by the pleasure brought on by Blade's determined pull. He stroked, suckling on her clit, his mouth pressing on the mound just above the nubbin. She hadn't realized that it, too, was a pleasure center. His keen, knowing pressure, combined with the pain, combined with his suckling, combined with the stroking of her G spot . . .

She screamed as the orgasm tore through her, letting out a flood of wetness.

Blade retreated, his expression smug . . . and gratified, she noticed. She reached for him, ignoring his hands, reaching instead for his hips. She only saw his smugness drop in surprise when she took his cock into her mouth, tracing the head with her tongue, quick as lightning. She took him as deep as she could without gagging. Turned on beyond belief, the orgasm still resonating through her system, she sucked gently, then twisted her face, stroking him in a gently gyrating motion. Using her saliva as lubricant, she stroked the rest of his impressive length with the slickness. She smiled around his girth when he made a low noise, his hips arching toward her.

Tom had moved behind her, and she heard the sound of a condom being rolled on. She wiggled her hips, eagerly, shamelessly. For the moment, all sense of purpose was gone. She was in the moment.

Alexis was right. Sex *was* power. And right now, Jelena was a goddess.

She was still sucking Blade when Tom entered her, his penetration eased by the juices of her previous orgasm. He was large, and gratifyingly broad, she realized with a moan of pleasure. He moved carefully, his cock tip circling her inner lips, his fingers still working her still-quivering clit. Then he eased himself in with a deep glide, and she moaned around

Blade's cock, gripping him hard. He growled, his hand knotting in her hair, holding her captive to him.

She moved away, shaking her head at him, and he looked at her with something between a sneer and a plea. She nudged him down on the bed, then moved between his legs. Tom moved with her, sinuously.

She was on all fours, hovering over Blade's enormous, tumescent erection, glistening from her attention. Tom covered her back, his hips against her ass, his cock buried deep in her pussy.

"*My* pleasure," she chastised Blade, and he closed his eyes as she massaged his cock between her breasts. Then Tom started to move, his hips pressing against hers, his hands pulling her flush against him. She spread her legs a little more, accommodating him. "Yes," she murmured. He was good . . . so large . . . so intent.

Blade made a growl of protest. She flashed a glare of her own at him.

He moved up, kneeling in front of her, cupping her breasts in his hands with almost painful insistence. He kissed her fiercely. His tongue tangled with hers, and she let him, pulling him roughly to her. The sensation of his hard, hot cock nestled against her stomach as Tom pressed inside her was thrilling. She nipped at Blade's lower lip. His moan in response, his kneading massage of her breasts, was enough to make her shudder with the pleasure of it.

Tom started moving faster, harder, his hand reaching between her body and Blade's, searching out and finding her clit. She moaned, leaning her head against Blade's shoulder, meeting Tom's every thrust with an equal backward thrust of her own as Tom's hand massaged her clit mercilessly. She was muttering incoherently now, writhing between the two men's bodies, sweat starting to dew over her skin. "I want you," she said. "God, I want you *both*."

Tom stopped, and she cursed. "Can you?" he breathed.

It took a moment to understand what he was asking. "No," she said, feeling some of her pleasure ebb. "Not . . . no. I've never . . ."

He reached between them. Sweat slicked, he parted her buttocks, his finger probing gently.

She tensed, pulling away from him, pushing even closer to Blade. He was large, but not as large.

"It can be enjoyable," Blade whispered now, his voice surprisingly gentle against her ear.

She froze. She knew what they were proposing.

No. Not this. Nothing was worth this. She could enjoy sex, even with two men, but she was not so far gone as to . . .

Before she could stop him, Tom pressed a little deeper. It was uncomfortable, but not horribly so.

"It would impress her," Tom said, but she sensed the reluctance in his voice.

She bit her lip. Thought about it. Closed her eyes.

"Take me," she said, then repeated it even more loudly. "Both of you. *Take me*."

It had been less than twenty-four hours, and he already felt like he was losing his mind without Nadia.

She's not coming back.

He would have to hunt her down. The thought sent adrenaline pulsing through his bloodstream. *Hunt her, find her, capture her.* Punish her, in such a way that she was screaming with pleasure. At least then, he knew, she wouldn't be contemplating leaving again. As long as she was mindless, lost in the release of the physical, she wouldn't consider life outside of his home . . . which was exactly what he wanted, because he wasn't letting her go, ever again.

God, you're fucked up.

He closed his eyes, sitting in the dark in his room. He glanced at the fireplace, at the mantel of his private bedroom suite, at the ornate clock. Ten o'clock at night.

Max made a little whimper, pacing.

"She's not coming back tonight, boy," Dominic replied, figuring out the source of Max's anxiety. He'd gotten used to her staying, sleeping in Dominic's bed, becoming a part of their house routine. She even gave him his treat at night. Max didn't like change.

Neither do I. And she might not be coming back at all.

Dominic stood up, stripping down, climbing into bed. One day, he'd given her, he swore to himself. One day. After she broke her promise on that, he'd be within his rights to go and bring her back. Drag her back, if need be—she'd given her word, too, after all, and he had a reputation to maintain. But he *had* to keep his word, no matter how he felt, or else he really would be The Beast, as everyone claimed he was.

She had asked for a day. He wanted to give her anything she asked for.

Anything except her freedom.

He winced as conscience slashed at him like a razor. She was growing to care for him. She seemed to like him. And she certainly liked making love to him—*having sex*, he corrected himself. He'd been open about his sexual practices, and he felt like he'd introduced her to a whole new level of pleasure. Of course, her innocent acceptance had taken him to a whole new level as well.

He could make her care for him. He would offer her anything in the world if she would only stay. And if she didn't want to . . . well. He'd just work harder.

That's not fair.

"Fuck fair," he said to himself, tossing heavily in the empty king-sized bed. He didn't care if it was fair or not. He had never responded to a woman the way he had to Nadia, not ever. He'd never experienced the joy that he had with her. He was a selfish bastard, and he wasn't ever going to let her go.

He was still telling himself that when he heard the door open.

Instantly, he grabbed for the gun that was mounted on the wall by his bed. His eyes adjusted to the darkness. He saw Max tense as well.

After a moment of sniffing the air, Max relaxed, resting his head back on the carpet.

"It's me," a soft voice cautioned him.

"Nadia," he breathed, relief flooding through his body.

She walked over, stripping off clothes as she made her way to the bed. She crawled under the covers with him, pressing her naked body against his. He enveloped her in his arms.

"You're crushing me," she said, with a breathless laugh.

Contrite, he immediately eased off. *I missed you.* Though of course, he would not say that. "I wanted you," he said instead, kissing her neck, her jaw. Then her mouth, thoroughly and passionately, loving the little gasp of pleasure she made against his lips. "You came back early." He was stunned by this. "Were you afraid I'd come after you?" He tried not to think about how appealing that plan had been.

"No, of course not. You gave your word."

She wasn't mocking him. She actually scoffed at his question.

"I'm not complaining," he said carefully, "but why are you back early?"

She was silent, still against him, and he sensed something was wrong. "I wanted you, too," she said, although she didn't mean it the way he meant it, he felt quite sure. There was something more complicated in the way she said it—some note of sadness.

He stroked her cheek. "What happened?"

She sighed, leaning against his palm, as if trying to get comfort from him. Then she snuggled against his chest. He was floored by her trust. He couldn't remember the last time someone had come to him for comfort. He hoped he wasn't screwing it up.

"My family is complicated," she replied softly. Then she propped herself up, looking into his eyes in the dim light. "Do you think it's wrong that my father has survived off of the money he's gained from—well, selling his daughters?"

His grip unintentionally tightened, and he forced himself to focus, not to hurt her. He thought her father was a coward and a bastard for selling his daughter . . . but that hadn't stopped him from buying her. It was a delicate balance.

"I know I've done enough shit in my life to probably be the least qualified to judge somebody," he said slowly. He kissed her, behind her earlobe, in the sensitive spot that made her shiver. "Whatever else I can say about your father, I can definitely say I'm glad he stole my car."

"Your Ferrari?" She let out a surprised laugh. "You weren't glad at the time."

"That was before I met you," he said. "You're worth a hundred of those cars. More."

She stared at him silently for a long moment. "You mean that," she breathed.

"I don't think your father's right in taking money from you, especially if it meant giving you to men who mistreated you. Part of me would gladly kill him for that. But they are your family." He shrugged. "You love them. I can't change that."

He held his breath. He hadn't meant to be that needy, that vulnerable. But he did desperately want to know her reasoning.

There was a long moment of silence.

"My sister thinks that I'm addicted to abuse."

"*What?*" He sat up, incensed. "She thinks I abuse you?"

"She doesn't know you, really," Nadia said quickly. "She thinks that I'm just . . . rolling over, giving in to whatever you want. Acting like your slave. She doesn't understand . . ."

"Doesn't understand what?" Dominic felt furious, almost nauseous with it. He wanted to kill her sister.

"How much I care about you."

Just like that, his emotions changed again. It was a damned roller coaster.

She reached for him, and his emotions changed yet again. She kissed him, not just with passion, but with . . . he couldn't describe it.

No game-playing tonight. His desire for her, mixed with the powder keg of emotions, was too volatile for something like that. He pressed his naked body to hers, his mouth finding hers in the darkness. He'd know her taste if he were separated from her for a thousand years. His tongue stroked the side of hers, caressing it as he savored the feel of her breasts dragging across his chest, her soft palms smoothing over his shoulders. One leg hooked over his hip, and his cock sprang to readiness. He adjusted himself, easing his way inside her. He slid into her snug passage like coming home, and he groaned against her lips. She sighed into his mouth, and her hips swiveled enough to tighten the small circlet of muscles enveloping the base of his shaft. He shuddered against her, tugging at her knee, drawing her closer. Pushing himself deep enough to feel his balls fit snug against her ass.

Slowly, sinuously, they rocked against each other, each tiny caress a masterpiece of ecstasy. Nothing hurried, or frantic. A murmur of pleasure here, a fraction of movement as their hips swayed apart, then together, then apart. She rippled against him. He cupped her breast in one palm as he tugged her hip with the other. She rolled against him, throwing her head back, her slight, breathless sighs urging him to go even slower, to revel in every frozen moment.

He'd never had this before, this kind of closeness. He

wanted to feast on her, yes, but nights like these, he just wanted to have her, slow and tight and reverent.

She shuddered against him in orgasm, and he shivered but stopped himself from joining her. He slid out, turning her over, then covered her like a blanket, entering her from behind. Still slow, still languorous, he withdrew his cock slowly until only the tip remained, then moved forward, like a yoga pose, until he was buried flush against her bottom. Sweat lubricated their bodies, and he slid over her with each movement. She gasped softly as he pressed deeper, her hands bunching in the sheets, her hips lifting up to meet his relentlessly slow thrusts.

"Dominic," she breathed. "Oh, my God . . ."

He couldn't speak, every ounce of control focused on her body. He kept up his strokes, holding her hips, pulling her tighter against him.

She cried out again, and he felt her body clench around him. He gritted his teeth until he thought he'd grind them into powder. He went completely still, until the aftershocks subsided.

Then he turned her, yet again, resting one of her heels against his shoulder. He penetrated her even more deeply this way, and he felt her embrace his entire length, slick with the fluid of her climaxes. He moved carefully, his hips moving like a tango dancer. He'd always felt too large and too brutish to be particularly graceful, but making love with Nadia was like Tai Chi, something almost beautiful in and of itself, without any end result.

She made the low, throaty sounds he loved, and her matching balletic movements seemed to caress and massage his already engorged cock past the point of endurance. Knowing he couldn't hold on much longer, he reached down, circling her clit, rubbing it with firm but gentle circles as his tempo increased inexorably, his hips starting to move with a rougher, uncontrolled force.

When she came again, he let her shuddering contractions milk him to his own release. He didn't shout, or groan. Instead, he silently shook, his hips jerking as his body emptied itself inside her. Then he lowered her leg, lowering himself onto her. He kissed her deeply, and she held him as he did.

Finally, he curled around her, sleep fogging his brain. He wasn't sure when he'd felt happier. He didn't care. It was enough to have her back.

"I wanted to come home to you, Dominic," she whispered, as he started to fall asleep.

"I always want you to come home to me," he replied, not thinking. "I love you."

He felt sleep close in around him, just as his conscience whispered treacherously:

Wait a minute. What did you just say?

Chapter Eleven

"Impressive performance," Alexis said to Jelena.

Jelena didn't answer. She looked instead around Alexis's office. It was quietly luxurious, tasteful. Especially considering it was the executive workspace for a brothel.

How did a woman like this get here? Why?

"You're obviously a determined woman, and after doing some research, I don't think you're working with the police." Alexis steepled her fingers, pressing them against her lower lip. "You said you want my help. What do you think I can do for you?"

"My sister," Jelena said. "You can help me rescue her, and get revenge on the man who's holding her captive."

"Really." Alexis drew out the word, her tone mocking. "How altruistic of me. And why will I be doing this?"

"The man that's holding her is Dominic Luder."

Alexis's body stiffened as if someone had snapped a whip across her back. Her normally guarded expression displayed a moment of naked fury for a second, before she was able to regain her composure. "I can't get to Dominic Luder," she said, and the anger and frustration at that fact simmered and seethed through every syllable.

"I think I can."

Jelena had her. Alexis was still as a statue, studying her with rapt attention. "How?" she asked, with cold eagerness.

Jelena outlined her plan, quickly. Alexis nodded, her eyes alight. "And your sister—what makes you think you can get her out so easily?"

"He dotes on her," Jelena said. "For now, anyway. I think he's trying to win her over, convince her he's some kind of . . . *good guy.*" She spat the words out.

"Oh he does, does he?"

If Jelena didn't know better, the vicious tone of voice would sound like jealousy. But this woman hadn't been with Dominic for years—by all accounts, she hated him. *Didn't she?*

It didn't matter. If it was more fuel for the fire, so be it. Jelena wanted Dominic dead.

"Your sister will hate you for interfering," Alexis added, nonchalant. "Are you sure she will go through with this?"

"She will," Jelena said. "I know my sister."

"Fine." Alexis's smile was bloodthirsty, at complete odds with her sophisticated surroundings, and for a second Jelena was actually afraid of her. "It's a bargain, then."

Jelena stood up, nodding. "It's a bargain."

As she saw her palm in the other woman's hand, she wondered, briefly, how a submissive little mail-order bride from Moscow could have come to this. Become this.

Then when she met Alexis's eyes, she thought she saw a foretaste of what she would become.

She gripped harder, but she didn't back away.

He'd told her he loved her. He hadn't meant for her to know, but now that he'd said it, now that it stood between them, she felt it like a surreal blessing. She'd never been in love before, not really. And she loved him. She loved his flaws, his faults. She loved the fact that he was blustery, but that he never wanted to hurt her. That he tried so hard to do what he felt was right. The way he took care of Max. The way he thought he wasn't good enough, with his scars. He was complicated, but then, so was she.

She loved him. And she needed to tell him.

They were sitting on the couch by the fireplace in the large living room. It was "their" place, she thought, with Max curled up at their feet. She was snuggled against Dominic's chest, gazing into the flames as he stroked her hair.

"What'll we do today?" he said against the crown of her head. "What do you want to do?"

He asked that, all the time—as if he were still worried that she might be unhappy, or bored. "I don't know. Go to a movie?"

"I've got a million movies here," he protested mildly. "Anything I don't have, I can order."

"It's not the same." She smiled hesitantly. "We could go

out to lunch, or maybe dinner. And a movie." There. That sounded normal, didn't it?

His answering smile was rueful. "My last outing to a public restaurant really didn't work out that well."

Abruptly, she remembered his knife wound. She stiffened, aghast. "You can't really leave at all, can you?"

We really can't leave at all.

She didn't say it out loud. She didn't have to.

"Not on a whim," he replied. "I need to be careful, plan my outings, think escape routes and contingencies. This house is safest."

"You're trapped here," she whispered. *We're trapped here.*

He shook his head. "It's only a prison if you want to get out." He stroked her body, cupping her breast in one palm. "I've got everything I want, right here."

He loves me, she thought, turning her face, brushing a quick kiss against his chest. But something gnawed at her.

"Are you going to have this hit or contract, or whatever, on you forever?"

His eyes darkened. "Alexis was a vengeful woman. I doubt she's suddenly going to have a change of heart. And she's got enough money, connections, and temper that it's not going to go away by anything that I do."

Nadia bit her lip, feeling her stomach sink. "Do you think she knows about me?"

His expression turned fierce. "Not if I can help it." Then he shrugged bitterly. "But you can see why I feel better as long as you're here, in the house."

She felt a slight grip of claustrophobia, despite the spaciousness of the mansion. After all, she did love him. But the thought of staying here, day after day, year after year. Would it be enough?

She sighed. *Having him would be enough,* she thought. *Yes. Of course it would.*

Are you trying to convince yourself?

"I guess you'd rather not see a movie, then," he said gently, and she swore he could read her thoughts.

"It's a little unnerving," she admitted.

"I should have just killed Alexis when I had the chance," he said, and she was surprised—and aghast—to hear him admit it. Especially since she'd brought it up before. "Sometimes I think she wants me dead so she won't have to worry about whether or not I'm planning some kind of elaborate retaliation against her."

Nadia swallowed hard. "Are you?"

He stroked her cheek, and his scarred face was gentle. "Not anymore. I've got more important things to think about."

That warmed her, seeping through her like an electric blanket. "And there's no way of telling her this?"

"No way she'll believe." He frowned. "I realize now she's not really capable of love, not the way I understand it. I don't think explaining it to her would work."

Love. There it was again. She smiled. *I love you, I love you . . .*

"Of course, she's only well connected in this country," he said slowly. "If you'd like to get out more, maybe we could move."

Nadia blinked. "Move? You mean . . . what do you mean?"

"I'd thought about it casually for a few years, but I'd already built this house like a fortress, and I guess I was too stubborn to leave." His voice was slow and thoughtful. "She's got some family connections in Europe, but not in Russia. You're from there, after all. Maybe . . ."

Nadia stiffened. "*No.* I'm not going back there."

The pain was evident in her voice. He sighed heavily. "I'm sorry. That was stupid." He paused. "Someplace else, then. Australia."

Nadia bit her lip. Australia. It seemed like a beautiful country. But . . . "Could she just as easily send someone there? To kill you, I mean?"

"She could," he admitted. "Not as easily, but not impossible. I'd want to build another house, something like this. Get to know the surroundings. It's not a perfect solution, but we'd have a little more freedom, especially if she didn't know. Or maybe I could fake our deaths, we could go and they'd never find out . . ."

"Fake our deaths?" Nadia blinked. "What about my family?"

He took a deep breath. "I'd make sure that a sizable amount was left to your father in my will."

Which didn't answer her question—and did. "I couldn't talk to them again."

"Not if we wanted to be safe." He paused. "You asked if you thought it was right for him to use you. I don't think so. And if you asked me, then you don't think so, either."

She bit her lip, hard, surprising herself that she didn't taste blood. "That doesn't mean I want to cut myself off from them completely."

"I know," he said. "But for your own safety—and maybe even theirs—don't you think it would be best?"

She blinked back tears at the thought. *For your own safety.* Why not do something completely selfish, just for herself? After all, she didn't need to live solely for their survival. She'd wanted a life of her own for so long.

But was she really trading it for a life of her own . . . or was she trading it for Dominic's life? Was she trading one servitude for another?

Damn you, Jelena.

"We don't need to talk about this right now," Dominic said gently, as if sensing the way her wayward thoughts were going. "What do you want to do?"

She closed her eyes. "I want you to make love to me."

"I have no problem with that, whatsoever."

When he reached for her, she stopped him. "I think I'd like to play a little game, this time."

He paused. "Are you sure?"

"Absolutely." Her voice rang with need.

He left for a moment, returning with a few items. His eyes gleamed as he took off his clothes.

"Turn around and lean against the couch, Nadia," he instructed, eagerness rippling through every syllable.

She got up, bending over the back of the leather couch. She spread her legs slightly, glancing at him over her shoulder. "Like this?" she purred.

He turned all the lights off, so the leaping flames were the only illumination in the room, throwing long shadows of the two of them on the walls. Then he studied her position. He produced a wine-colored velvet blindfold. She stayed perfectly still as he tied it around her head. The world was reduced to sound, scent. Physical sensation.

Don't forget taste.

She could hear him move around her, then heard the leather creak as he moved on the cushions. The velvety tip of his cock stroked against her lips, and she licked at him, playfully at first, then more intently, taking him into her mouth and suckling him, her tongue stroking the underside of his shaft. She heard his groan and shivered, her pussy going slick with anticipation.

He pulled away, and she still heard the rustling noises of his moving around. He tugged at her wrists, pulling them behind her. She felt the silken tassels bind loosely around her wrists.

"You'll enjoy this," he whispered in her ear. "We both will."

She felt him spread her legs wider, until she felt the air against her exposed labia. She moaned softly against the back of the couch as he worked her vulva with his fingers, circling her sensitive opening, teasing her clit and retreating.

He gave her a quick, flicking spank. She was ready for it, but she still squealed lightly in surprise. He laughed, a low, short sound.

He continued stroking her, until her hips twitched and her pussy clenched with need. Then, like clockwork, another quick, lightly stinging spank. Until she felt his hot breath between her thighs, his tongue delving into her folds, circling her clit. He pressed a finger inside her, then another, and she moaned more loudly, going up on tiptoe to press herself more firmly against his feasting mouth. She was breathing in short, shallow breaths, and he circled her clit with his thumb, massaging it, until she was on the brink of coming.

Then, with his free hand, he spanked her. She let out a little shriek, then a little moan.

He withdrew his fingers completely, and she let out a cry of indignation. "Dominic . . ."

"This first." He plunged his cock in, hot and fast and rough, and she yelled, feeling her cunt clamp around him like a vise. He reached around, gripping at her breasts as he pumped against her. She arched her back, then pressed herself insistently backward, impaling herself on his thick, hard cock. It felt sensational. He moaned loudly as he pulled her against him, slamming against her with force, and she moved like a mating animal. Her arms were trapped between them, she was powerless and tied up and gloried in it.

Her orgasm shot through her, and she gasped as her body shimmered with it.

He pulled out, and she felt that moment of being bereft again as he untied her hands. She was surprised, then, when he picked her up, carrying her.

"Where are you taking me?"

He didn't answer. When she repeated the question, he nipped at her, and the fire in her pussy redoubled. She didn't know what he was going to do—she couldn't see. She was still in his power.

She held on to him and waited.

She heard a door unlock as they approached, and he opened it. The room smelled faintly stale, the air a little stagnant. What was this place? It was air-conditioning cool, and there was the scent of plastic. Maybe vinyl.

He put her down on what felt like a padded table. Soft, mink-lined restraints were buckled into place around her wrists, her ankles. Her skin felt so alive, she might be glowing.

The restraints forced her legs wider, wider still, almost to the point of discomfort. She still couldn't see. The cool air made her nipples hard as pebbles.

"Dominic?" Her voice held a slight quaver, and she felt a moment of uneasiness.

He stepped between her splayed thighs. The table lowered a little, and then she felt his cock, nuzzling at the entrance of her pussy. He leaned forward, laving her breasts, groaning as he entered her already damp cunt. He stroked every inch of her, maddening caresses she couldn't return. Her whole world was narrowed down to the feel of him on her. She rolled her head from side to side as he plunged and withdrew, plunged and withdrew, burying himself inside her fully and retreating.

His breathing sped up, and she felt excitement merging with the fear, coopting it, taking over her. He was almost snarling as he pumped against her, and she was practically chanting with need, unintelligible words of heat and desire, her body arching with each thrust inside her. She was losing her mind. She didn't care.

Shouting with triumph and satisfaction, he slammed against her, his hips flush against her thighs, his cock buried deep as it jerked and released his cum. She screamed his name as she shuddered in response, her body convulsing around him. Her mind went completely, momentarily, blank.

This was what she wanted. She didn't want to be in charge. She didn't want to have to make the decision. As long as she was following someone else's plan, she didn't have to take any responsibility for her unhappiness.

Oh, God.

Her eyes widened at the thought.

He was slumped over the table, sated, sweaty. He kissed her breasts, her throat, her lips. "I love you," he rasped.

"I love you, too, Dominic," she said softly, meaning every word.

His voice had been broken and hopeful and she felt like a knife had been driven into her chest.

I love you, she thought. *But I have no idea how to make this work.*

I want to stay like this forever.

Dominic couldn't remember the last time he'd felt this content. Nadia was tucked up against his chest on the couch as they stared into the fire. They'd made love, had lunch, and were just hanging out. They had no plans and no urgency to create any.

He felt . . . God, he felt *happy,* he realized. And just as abruptly felt a chill of dread cover him.

As a result, he jumped when his cell phone rang, then frowned at his own foolishness. His brow furrowed as he read the number: no one he recognized, someone from Las Vegas. He should let it ring through to voicemail and take Nadia instead. Still, something in the base of his spine twitched. Few people had his private number. If it wasn't a mistake, then it was probably something important. Hell, maybe it was someone telling him that Alexis had died in a tragic accident, or perhaps she'd run off to become a Buddhist nun—either way, lifting the contract from him.

He glanced at Nadia, who was scratching Max behind the ears. He could believe in fairy tales, now.

He answered the phone with a suspicious "Hello?"

"I must speak to Nadia. Immediately."

The sister. She must have kept the number when Nadia called her about their half brother's birth. He handed over the phone. "I think it's Jelena."

"My sister?" Nadia said, sounding stunned, and reached for the phone. "Hello?"

He couldn't make out the exact words, but the sister's voice was shrill, her words quick and in Russian.

"What? Why?" Nadia sat up, her back stiffening. Her grip on the cell phone was hard. "What's wrong?" Her face turned pale as her sister's voice grew higher pitched, her words even faster.

"What's happened? Ill? How? When?"

Dominic felt ice creep through his stomach. Something was wrong . . . hideously wrong. He wanted to comfort her, but wasn't sure how.

Nadia looked at Dominic helplessly. "I don't know," she whispered. "I don't know if I can . . ."

Dominic gritted his teeth, hard enough for his jaw to bulge. She had to leave. Her sister was telling her she had to leave.

The look of anguish on her face, the look of torn despair, gnawed at him.

"I don't even know where the family's house is," she protested. "Is papa in the hospital? Where . . ." She fell silent again, then shot another look over at Dominic. The sister was saying something about him, that much was obvious. "All right. All right. I'll see what I can do."

She closed the phone without so much as a goodbye, handing it back to him. He could see the tears forming in her eyes.

"What happened?" he asked quietly, taking his phone and tucking it in his pocket.

"My father. He's sick—he's dying."

"Of what?" The *timing* of it, damn it . . .

"She didn't have time to say. She only said it was happening quickly, and Dominic, she sounded so scared . . ." The pain in Nadia's voice was clear.

"You want to go to him."

"I don't want to leave you," she said softly. "But . . ."

"I know. He's your father. It's your family." Logically, he knew that. Still, he scowled, unable to resist adding, "She wouldn't say what was wrong? It sounds suspicious to me."

"She was frantic," Nadia defended.

He just bet. That sister, Jelena, seemed just as treacherous as the old man—more so, maybe, because Nadia couldn't see it. Everything about this smelled like a trap.

He looked into Nadia's hazel eyes, ready to stand his ground. If her father was dying . . .

"If he wanted to see you that badly, he should've thought of it before letting you pick up the tab on something he did wrong," Dominic said, feeling desperate.

Nadia sighed, looking at him with reproach. "You don't understand."

"I understand that you'll let them keep hurting you until you snap."

She stood up, hurt etched on her face. "What he's done—what I've *let* him do—isn't right," she said, with a quiet dignity that shamed him down to his soul. "But he's still my father, and I still love him. I want to see him before he dies."

"How can you love someone like that?"

How could she love someone like me?

"Love's funny," she said, her eyes growing tender, tears finally spilling over and trailing down her cheeks. She stepped up to him, stroking his scarred cheek. Instinctively, he curved his face into her palm, nuzzling her. He'd never had anyone treat him so well, even when he was still handsome. She touched him like he was something precious.

He was bending, he knew it. The thought scared him, sickened him.

"Where are you going to see him?"

"I'm supposed to go to Jelena's," she said, and distrust leaped to the fore again. "She'll take me to see him."

"You couldn't even get an address from her?"

She blushed. "She was afraid that you'd . . ." She let the statement peter out.

"She was afraid I'd come, kill your father," he said, and he sighed wearily. That made sense, more sense than anything else. Jelena didn't trust him, and she was right not to. She wasn't as trusting as her sister.

Of course, she didn't know he was in love with her sister.

He closed his eyes. "It means a lot to you, doesn't it?"

He felt her sit on his lap, hugging him. "It would mean a lot to me, yes," she murmured. "And I promise you, I will come back."

He shuddered. There was something wrong with this, something very wrong. But he had to learn to trust her, didn't he?

He nodded slowly. "All right." His voice was ragged. "Go where you need to go."

She hugged him tightly, fiercely. "I promise you, I'll come back."

"You'd better," he said, holding her to him, stroking her silken hair.

If you love something, set it free. He chuckled mirthlessly to himself. Whoever made that statement ought to get his ass kicked.

"Thank you," she breathed, then kissed him, gently. He could taste the salt from her tears, the sheer gratitude. "Thank you for trusting me."

I love you, he thought. He knew it. She knew it. What was once more.

He tried to force himself to say it. No words came out, even after she'd left the room.

Chapter Twelve

Nadia was surprised she didn't get pulled over on her way to Jelena's house. Dominic loaned her one of his fastest cars, and the Lamborghini drove so smoothly that she didn't notice she was going past a hundred miles an hour until she glanced down by accident. Nerves made her foot press reflexively harder on the gas pedal.

What's wrong with Papa? Why couldn't Jelena simply tell her? Had he gotten in trouble? Maybe shot? Who had he screwed over this time?

When was he going to grow up?

She zipped into Jelena's curving driveway, stopping short in front of her gate. She punched in the code by memory. For all she knew, her father was genuinely dying. It wasn't kind of her to blame her father for . . .

She grimaced at herself in the rearview mirror. For one brief moment, she didn't care if it was kind. She was getting tired of cleaning up his messes.

The gate swung open, and she drove up to the front door. By the time she got to it, Jelena was already there, opening it for her. She looked different, Nadia noticed, although the differences would probably only be noticeable to someone who knew Jelena well. Her clothing was different: no longer the pristine matched suits that pegged her as a society wife, she was wearing clothing that was a bit more clingy, a bit more revealing, if just as sophisticated. She seemed to be wearing a bit more makeup as well. No, not more . . . just *different.* Sexier. The overall effect was not one of seduction, however. If anything, Jelena was . . .

Nadia frowned. *Intimidating* seemed to be the only word that applied.

Since when had her pliant trophy sister been intimidating?

"It took you long enough," Jelena snapped, grabbing her by the arm and shutting the door behind her.

"Where's Papa? What happened?"

"Upstairs." Jelena followed her, typing in numbers hastily on a cell phone.

"He's here? Are you keeping them all here? What happened?" Nadia stopped, crossing her arms and scowling at her sister. "Damn it, what's going on?"

"What, are you on a time limit?" Jelena asked sharply. "Are you only allowed a few hours of freedom?"

"I'm asking about Papa, and you're still carping about

Dominic?" Nadia shot back. "Dominic loves me—and even if he didn't, he's not your problem. Don't worry about my life."

"Somebody needs to," Jelena said. "How does he trust you to get back in anyway? Does he wait at the gate or something?"

"What happened to Papa?"

Jelena's dark expression was one of muted fury. "Nothing's wrong with Papa."

It took Nadia a second to realize what had happened. "Jelena . . . tell me you didn't lie to me just to get me away from Dominic."

"I wouldn't have if I thought there were some other way to get you free from that prison. He doesn't let you leave. He doesn't let you *breathe*. And worst of all, you actually think you enjoy it!"

"This has nothing to do with you!" Nadia stormed.

"Really? Did you have to beg for him to let you loose? Do you honestly think if it hadn't been life-threatening, he would have ever let you go?"

"Right," Nadia said. "He hates father, and wanted to kill him . . . but he's enough of a soft heart to let me leave because the man's sick. Or so I thought. What do you think? Do you really think he's a bastard? What, are there rules I don't know about?"

Jelena's eyes were a little wild. Something was wrong. Something was terribly, terribly wrong.

"I'm not going to let you make the same mistakes I made," Jelena said, and her voice was frantic. Crazed. "I'm not going to watch you throw your life away for a man who doesn't deserve it. Who mistreats you and who should be made to pay for it!"

"What happened to you, Jelena?" Nadia asked softly, in Russian. "What's broken you this way?"

Jelena let out a short, barking laugh tinged with madness. "Does he let you have free run of the place, then? Are you the mistress of his house? Do you know the code to get back there, or do you have to ring him at the gate like a delivery woman?"

"It's not like that," Nadia said, feeling anger and fear mixing like gas and fire.

"What, are the gates simply wide open, then?"

Nadia huffed impatiently. "What difference does it make? The car," she snapped. "It's got something in it; I can get back in whenever I want. But that's not the point. I know it's his house, and his car, and I am just a guest. But he cares for me. We might not have the relationship I wanted, but nothing's perfect, and besides, that's my problem, not yours. I'll figure out what to do with it."

Jelena's expression softened slightly. "I can't watch you get hurt," she muttered. "I've stood by blindly for too long. I just . . . I can't bear it."

Nadia sighed, then reached out and hugged her sister. "I know," she breathed. "And I'm sorry. But, honestly, in this family, don't you think it's time we started letting each other make some mistakes, and learn from them?"

"You didn't let Papa learn from his mistakes."

"No. No, I didn't." And it had gotten her Dominic. But

even Dominic had not wanted her to pay that price. And now . . . "But it's the last time."

"Easy to say," Jelena scoffed.

"No. From now on, if someone makes a mistake, he's going to pay for it on his own."

Jelena eased herself out of Nadia's arms. "I'm glad you said that."

Then she shut her cell phone with a snap. Nadia stared at the phone, puzzled. "What was that?"

Jelena shook her head. "A friend. Someone who's going to help me."

There was the sound of tires squealing in the driveway. An engine roaring to life, then disappearing down the hill.

Nadia ran down the stairs, ice forming in the pit of her stomach. She threw open the door.

The Lamborghini was gone.

She turned back to Jelena. "What have you done?"

"Dominic Luder needs to pay for his mistakes, Nadia," she said, and her voice rang with a fierce sort of triumph. "And he's going to pay with his life."

"No!" Nadia felt panic, sharp as a razor, slice through her. "You've got to help me stop them!"

"What's the problem? He's a big boy. He can take care of himself."

I promise I won't leave you. I don't ever want to hurt you.

"He'll think I betrayed him," she said, feeling a greasy, nauseous panic churn in her stomach. "My God, if he dies . . ."

"Don't worry," Jelena said, finally calm. "You won't need to worry about him after this. He won't hurt you, no matter what he might think before he dies."

Nadia spun and slapped Jelena, hard enough to make her hair tumble around her shoulders. Jelena stared at her, cradling her face.

"*I love him.*" She screamed it. "You don't know his life, and I'm starting to realize . . . you don't know mine. He's been screwed over and maimed and he just wants to be left alone. He's tired of being attacked. I could have built a life with him and now you've ruined *all of that!*"

Jelena's expression was one of fascinated horror.

"Give me your keys," Nadia said.

"What?"

"Your car keys!" Nadia shoved Jelena back in the house. "I have to get to him. I have to stop this!"

"It's too late," Jelena said, her voice sounding numb. "You don't know the people who are after him."

"The people *you* sent," Nadia growled. "I don't even know you anymore. Now give me your damned keys!"

"No. You might get killed."

Nadia wanted to rip her hair out. "I will get there, don't worry," she said, walking toward the door. "And if anything happens to him, God help you, Jelena."

"I'm your family," Jelena said. "Does that mean nothing?"

Nadia stopped for one second, closing her eyes, feeling the years of pain and sacrifice and . . . and sheer *stupidity*, lashing at her, like a multitude of bruises.

"Just being family does not excuse this," she said. "I love

you. But I'm not going to let the people I love hurt me. Not anymore."

With that, she walked out the door and into the night.

Max kept sending looks to the door.

"Stop that," Dominic said, with no heat in his voice. "She'll come back. She promised."

Max whined softly, then took his place at Dominic's feet, curling up on the rug in front of the fireplace.

It had only been a few hours since Nadia had left. He'd been living like a hermit for, what, some three years since the explosion. It wasn't like he couldn't fill the time somehow. He was an intelligent man.

Of course, he was now a man in love. Apparently that had a few drawbacks—like a touch of obsession and a tendency to pine.

He gritted his teeth, heading to his computer. He'd see who was online at the forum, play some chess. See about increasing his ranking. No . . . chess gave him too much time to think, and in his current mental state, he'd probably get creamed by a fourth grader. Halo. He'd play Halo, shoot stuff. Get some of the viciousness out of his system.

Except he wasn't *feeling* viciousness anymore. It was just ache, longing, and—without her—loneliness.

God, he was pathetic.

Max looked toward the doorway, then in a flash was on his feet. Dominic heard the sound of a door opening.

"Nadia?" He couldn't stop himself from calling out.

There was the sound of footsteps. A lot of footsteps. Max's hackles rose and he snarled.

Shit. It definitely wasn't Nadia—although, technically, only Nadia had an access code ring.

Shit.

He got to his feet. Why didn't he have his gun with him? Why had he gotten so lax?

"Don't bother, Dominic," a familiar voice purred. "God, you're a mess. I keep forgetting just how extensive the damage was. You're not beautiful at *all* anymore, now, are you?"

"Alexis," he responded, feeling weariness seep into his bones. "Been a while."

Alexis stepped into his living room, surrounded by five garden-variety thugs. "Too long," she said, and her violet eyes glittered dangerously. "I should have gotten around to this years ago. I had no idea you'd be so difficult to kill."

"I've always had a strange talent for self-preservation," he agreed. "Even when I didn't give a shit about living. I'm not entirely sure how that worked out."

"It's not going to help you today," she snapped. "But don't worry. I wasn't planning on killing you quickly, anyway." She turned to her group of quasi-henchmen. "Take him out, but don't kill him. We're definitely going to hurt him first."

He sighed. This was going to be a pain in the ass.

Two of the thugs were just hired help; druggies, more than likely, from the manic look in their eyes and their gross overconfidence. Someone needed to teach these assholes that a couple of tattoos and a leather jacket didn't make you a badass. Dominic guessed he'd be the teacher of that particular lesson. But the other two . . . the first, a tall, pale blond man, thin and withdrawn, with a quiet studiousness that suggested he knew what he was doing. And the other, a short olive-skinned man with onyx eyes who looked like he'd like to make a career out of torturing people. Which, come to think of it, he probably had.

Problematic. But at least for a few minutes he wouldn't be thinking of . . .

"So tell me: who's Nadia?" Alexis asked, trying to sound bored but simply sounding jealous. "I certainly hope she didn't mean much to you."

Dominic's blood ran cold. Suddenly, his mind shifted into a crystalline clear focus.

The amateur thugs rushed him. As he suspected, they were clumsy, inept. He kicked their asses easily. One got knocked out. The other went running, much to Alexis's disdain.

"You should hire better help," Dominic suggested, not even winded.

"They couldn't all be you, Dominic," Alexis returned sourly.

"A compliment?" He shook his head, still keeping his eyes fixed on the other two combatants. "You're getting mellow, Lexy."

The dark-haired man giggled. Yes, *giggled*. Creepy little fucker, that one.

"You never did answer my question," she said. "Who's Nadia?"

"Little busy here, Alexis," he answered, as the blonde and

the short guy started to circle him. "Can I get back to you after I get rid of your other flunkies?"

The blonde produced a knife, the short guy a gun. Which meant taking the short guy out first. A knife wound he could live with. Even though the caliber on the gun didn't look like much, he'd rather not . . .

"Oh, wait," Alexis interrupted with exaggerated cheerfulness. "I know Nadia! She's the lovely girl I got your cute little Lamborghini from."

Her comment had the desired effect. He met her eyes for a moment, gauging her sincerity. Like a well-orchestrated maneuver, the blonde rushed him as the short guy shot him in the leg.

"*Fuck!*" he shouted as he toppled over like a demolished building. The two men pounced. He felt the blade at his neck as the short guy quickly and effectively bound his wrists and feet, hog-tying him.

"Careless," Alexis said, hovering in front of him. "This Nadia must've really meant something to you."

He didn't like her use of the past tense. "If you hurt her," he said, between gritted teeth, "I will personally make sure your last breaths are incredibly painful ones."

She knelt down, grinning evilly. "You aren't really in a position to make threats, you realize. But don't worry. I didn't hurt your little friend."

She was gearing up for something, he realized as the binding around his wrists tightened.

"I didn't have to," she added. "She gave me the car quite easily."

Pain stabbed at Dominic, and it had nothing to do with his restraints. "Nice try," he said, glad his voice was steady.

But how did *Alexis get the car?* His subconscious nagged at him. It probably wasn't that hard. Nadia was upset—thinking her father was dying. It'd be easy to boost it from her.

Or she betrayed you.

He ignored the internal chatter.

"You're so confident, then, that a spurned lover wouldn't be angry enough to want you dead?"

"Alexis, I've never said this, but . . . " He sighed. "I'm sorry."

Now she was the one to look shocked. The expression quickly shifted to wariness. "For what, exactly?"

"For leading you on," he said. "For not being what you wanted. Taking you for granted. Basically, for being an arrogant, egotistical ass."

She laughed, a brittle sound. "You don't honestly think that an apology this late in the game is going to change anything."

"No," he said. "But I still needed to say it."

She sent a quick, sharp look to the blonde. The blonde responded by kicking Dominic in the kidney. Pain radiated up through Dominic's back, and he let out a hiss.

"You deserve this," she said. "You may be sorry, but I don't forgive you."

He would have shrugged. If he had the freedom of movement anyway. Instead, he simply looked bored.

"Your Russian girlfriend agreed with me."

He was moving past bored, heading toward downright Zen. "You're lying," he said easily.

"Really? How do you know?"

Because she said she loved me. He didn't even bother to respond.

"Money changes everything," Alexis mocked. "I paid that little bimbo handsomely to finally get my hands on you, Dominic. And I'm going to make sure that you realize that for the few excruciating hours you've got left to live."

He shook his head.

"You don't believe you're going to die?" Alexis's voice rose in pitch, clearly agitated.

"I think I'm probably going to die," he said. "But I'll tell you one thing I know: Nadia would never betray me."

Funny, that it took this to clarify that statement. He was about to die, and he finally knew, with complete certainty, that he'd fallen in love with the one woman on earth he knew he could trust.

Nadia, I was an idiot.

Too bad he'd never get the chance to tell her.

Chapter Thirteen

He'll be fine. Isn't he always? He's the most untrusting, para-noid, lethal man you know.

Nadia's foot still pushed the accelerator of Jelena's BMW to the floor. When she got to his house, the gate was open, and she felt a pulse of panic hit her in the stomach. She zoomed up the driveway. There was a champagne-colored Hummer, complete with spinning rims, sitting in front of the door. Dominic would rather be dead than drive such a gaudy monstrosity.

The front door was wide open as well. A terrible, terrible sign.

She headed up the steps cautiously, her brain shifting in-stinctively to the same ice-cold rational mindset that she'd clicked into the first night she met Dominic. She crept through the front door into the dark, cavernous foyer.

There was the sound of raised voices, a woman's screeching orders in particular. "What will it take to get you to cry, big man?"

"Nothing you've got," came the slurred reply. *Dominic*, she thought, her heart pounding frantically in her chest. She headed toward the living room, hiding behind one of the stout maple beams. She peered around quickly, carefully.

What she saw made her stomach clench. Dominic was on the floor, tied at the hands and ankles. A blond man with what looked like a pipe was cracking on Dominic's tied legs with slow, deliberate precision. His expression was bored. With each heavy thud, Dominic winced, but did not make any sound otherwise. His eyes were swollen, turning black . . . blood seeped from his hairline. He looked like a trapped animal.

"So fucking tough," the woman—obviously Alexis—said with scorn. "Markus?"

A short, Mediterranean-looking man stepped out of the shadows, a scalpel in his hand and a look of unholy anticipation in his eyes.

"Tell me, was it worth it?" Alexis said, as the man approached Dominic's prone form.

Dominic grunted. "Which part?"

"Screwing me over," she said, and Nadia heard the edge of madness crackling in the woman's voice. "I loved you."

"No," Dominic said sadly. "You didn't."

It only infuriated Alexis more. "What the fuck would you

know about it? Who the *fuck* have you ever been in love with, besides yourself?"

He was quiet.

"Ah, so you think you were in love with that Nadia bitch, huh?" She kicked him in the forehead. "How many times do I have to tell you? She *betrayed* you. She sold your sorry ass out for a couple of grand!"

"She didn't." Dominic's voice was low, but the certainty in his voice was enough to warm her heart. "I know."

"Idiot," Alexis muttered. Then she stepped back. "I guess it's your turn, Markus. Carve him as slowly as you like. No-body's coming to save him." She turned to go.

"Don't you want to watch?" Markus said, sounding disappointed.

"Tell me if he starts crying or begging," she said. "Until then, I don't care. I'll be in the car."

Nadia was quiet as the tall woman swept past her hiding space, her face contorted with bitterness and rage. Nadia heard her high heels clicking like machine-gun fire on the granite tiles of the foyer. She waited until Alexis was outside, the door slamming behind her.

Nadia made her move.

She picked up a small, solid bronze statue. The blond man was closest. She could smell the smoke wafting from around the post. The other, Markus, had the scalpel to Dominic's back, muttering gleefully under his breath.

Limit your targets.

Silently, she moved around and clocked the blond man with all her strength, the statue's base hitting his temple. He let out a garbled, infuriated yell as he fell over. She kicked him in the balls, viciously, then hit him in the head again, harder. His eyes rolled back, and then his eyelids closed. She took the gun from his limp hand.

Dominic let out a snarl. When she looked up, the man had sliced into his shoulder. She held the gun on him.

"Drop it," she said.

He smiled. "Or what?"

She fired at him, deliberately missing, the bullet whizzing past his ear and embedding itself in the wall. She adjusted her aim, goading him.

He grimaced at her, putting down the scalpel. Then, almost too quickly to see, he drew a tiny gun out of nowhere, shooting at her. She shot back, nailing him in the shoulder. Yowling in pain, he fled, dripping blood.

She rushed to Dominic's side. "Are there more of them?" She was all but shaking with the overload of adrenaline in her system, but the small, sane part of her forced her to be practical. She'd break down later. Once she knew Dominic was safe.

He was staring at her. "I must be hallucinating."

"More of them?" she prodded.

"No," he chuckled softly. "You're real. Only my Nadia would get pissed at me for not staying focused."

She sliced through the cords with the scalpel. He rolled to his back, groaning with pain.

A shot rang through, and she held her gun up to meet the new threat. Alexis was back, this time with her own weapon.

"Don't tell me," she said sourly. "You're the infamous Nadia."

Nadia kept her gun trained on the tall woman, and stayed silent.

"You don't look a bit like your sister," Alexis noted. "Do you have any idea what she did, to get me here?"

Nadia still didn't answer. She kept the woman in her sights.

"If you leave now, you don't have to get hurt," Alexis said. "I don't give a shit about you. I just want him."

"So do I."

Alexis made a little expression of disgust. "Isn't that romantic? I suppose you love him, too."

Nadia's finger tensed on the trigger.

"He's a beast. A monster," Alexis said. "He's only let me live to torture me with the thought that, someday, he'd kill me painfully. Every day is a nightmare."

"I promise, I won't kill you," Dominic said, surprising Nadia by slowly getting to his knees. "I won't do anything to you. It's over. And I'm sorry for the past."

"*Shut up!*" The gun in Alexis's hand shook. "Nothing you say will ever make up for what you've done to my life! You don't understand!"

Nadia's arms were beginning to tire from holding the gun upright so long. She had to change the situation. She had to . . .

"But you're going to understand," Alexis said, and the gun changed position. Now, it aimed directly at Nadia. "Because you're finally going to lose something you care about."

"*No!*"

The gun went off. Nadia's finger pulled, the gun kicking back in her palm.

Alexis's expression was one of stunned, irritated disbelief. The bullet caught her in the throat. Blood sprayed in a fine mist, and Alexis toppled to the floor.

The shock and horror of what had just happened would sink in later. Right now, Nadia tried to stay calm. She didn't feel anything—not the numbness of shock, not the pain of a bullet wound. Immediately, she looked at Dominic.

He looked pale. Too pale.

He was her target. He was the one Alexis had hit with her last bullet.

"Dominic," she breathed, trying to hold him, trying to figure out where the bullet was lodged. "Dominic, please hang on."

He smiled at her, a tender, lopsided smile that shattered what little control she had left. She started to tremble, crying.

"I knew you wouldn't betray me," he said softly. "I do trust you, Nadia. And I do love you."

"I love you, too," she said, pressing kisses against his cheek. His skin was cold, clammy with shock. She tried to warm him. "You can't die now."

He grimaced. "I'm working on that."

She held him close as she heard the sound of sirens, echoing down the hallway. She knew he'd probably hate it, but she was glad she'd called the police as she rushed over here.

"Don't worry about anything," she murmured, kissing him gently. "I've got you."

He breathed a soft word, as the EMTs and police crashed down the hallway. She couldn't make it out. "What was that?" she said, leaning close to his mouth.

His lips caressed her earlobe.

"Forever," he said. "You've got me forever."

Chapter Fourteen

Nadia was sitting in a different lobby of the same hospital where Deidre had given birth. Now she waited to hear how Dominic was faring. She felt an edge of anxiety, realizing how close she was to losing him.

Jelena, Irina, and her father walked in. Her father embraced her, looking puzzled. "I left Deidre home with the baby. Tell me, why are we here?"

"Papa," she said, feeling her throat catch, "Dominic's been hurt."

"What does it matter?" Jelena said, although Nadia noticed that her eyes widened at *hurt*. "You were his prisoner. He deserves everything he gets, and then some."

"Whatever you need to tell yourself, Jelena," Nadia said coolly, "we both know the truth."

Jelena flushed. Her father cleared his throat.

"You feel something for this man, then."

"Papa, I love him."

He looked a little bewildered. "How? A man like . . ." At her stern stare, he let the statement peter off. "And he feels . . . ?"

"He loves me, too, Papa."

He sighed heavily. "Well, at least some good has come from this," he said, after a long pause. "When he feels better, we'll negotiate with him."

"*No.*" That, from Jelena.

Nadia shook her head, as well. "I am going to be with him, but it's not an arrangement. It has nothing to do with the family."

Her father turned scarlet, right up to the roots of his hair. "Wait a minute. You're choosing this man, this stranger, over your own family?" He sounded incensed. "You'll take bread out of your baby brother's mouth, just for your own selfish pleasure?"

"I'm choosing to have my own life," Nadia countered. "I love him, and I want to be with him. It has nothing to do with my baby brother, or my sisters. Or you, Papa."

"You're my daughter," her father said with menace.

"You don't own us, father!" Jelena snapped. "You never did!"

He glanced around nervously. "This is not the place to have this conversation. We'll go home." He turned to leave.

"Papa, I'm not going home."

He turned back to Nadia. "Come home *right now.*"

"That isn't going to work," Nadia said sadly. "I love you, and I will always do what I can to help you. But I'm not going

to just be a bargaining chip for you anymore, Papa. I'm finished. I'm not a meal ticket. I'm your daughter, and you need
to love me and respect me for what I am."

"Of course I love you," he said, looking bewildered. "What
does that have to do with anything?"

She looked at Jelena. He didn't understand. He really, genuinely didn't understand.

Jelena sighed. "Perhaps you should go home, Papa."

Now he looked at them, aghast at the mutiny taking place.
"You lead her to this," he accused. "You're divorcing your
husband, and you're talking about not remarrying. You've
made money with a settlement with him somehow, and
you're keeping me cut out of it! What is this?"

"I'm taking control of my own finances," Jelena said, and
there it was again—that intimidating quality. She sounded
like a general.

"You're a woman," her father said caustically. "How could
you . . ."

"Papa," Jelena said, her voice sharp enough to cut steel.
"You don't want to cross me on this. I promise you."

Her father gasped. Jelena didn't blink.

"I thought I was protecting you," Jelena said to Nadia. "I
did everything I could to stop you from making these mistakes. I'm not sorry."

"You will be if you try it again." Nadia stood up to her
sister, infusing every word with menace. "I mean it. Leave
Dominic and me alone."

Jelena shrugged. "If you're going to be stupid enough to
stay, I can't stop you. I can only save myself."

"What the hell is going on here?" her father asked plaintively. "You're crazy! You've both gone crazy! Turning against your family, turning against each other, for what? What the hell is wrong with you?"

"I'm not going to be your whore any more, Father," Jelena said, her voice ringing with finality.

"And I'm just going to be your daughter from now on," Nadia said more gently. "I'm staying with Dominic, because I love him."

Jelena shook her head, but at least she seemed to realize there was nothing she could say that would dissuade Nadia. It was the way it was.

Her father was finally deflated, at a loss. "It's all falling apart," he muttered. "You're all abandoning me."

"It's not about you," Jelena snapped.

Nadia gripped his hand.

"Many marriages are unhappy. I was unhappy. Arrangements aren't for love, they are for survival. I thought you girls understood that." He stared at her pleading. "We had to make sacrifices to survive."

"Yes, we did," Nadia said. "But I don't have to. Not anymore. And neither does Jelena."

He set his jaw. Then he nodded.

"We'll just have to make do, then," he said, sounding disappointed. "With the new baby, and your sister Irina . . . what will we do?"

"You'll do what you have to," she said, as sympathetically as possible. "No new cars. Take care of that baby."

"I dreamed of so much more than this," he mused.

"So did I," she answered.

He didn't, couldn't, understand. Nadia felt an ache in her heart. She kissed his cheek goodbye. "I'll call soon."

She did dream of more than this. Now she had a chance at it, and she wasn't going to lose that.

The doctor came out, and she stood. "You can see Mr. Luder now."

"How is he?"

"Much better. A tough, er, guy." She got the feeling he was about to say something else, like *bastard*, but had thought the better of it. "He has a tremendous will to live, and that helps matters immensely. He'll be weak for a while, he'll need to recover. But I don't see why he shouldn't be much healthier in a few months."

"Thank you," she breathed, then followed him impatiently into the room.

Dominic lay there, his scarred face pale, tubes attached to him, IVs. The doctor left them alone.

"I was so worried I'd lose you," she said, taking his hand and squeezing it hard.

He smiled, her favorite lopsided smile. His eyes were serious. "So now what are we going to do?"

She smiled. "You're going to be in here for a little while. I'll stay for as long as they let me. Then, they'll let you go home. I'll take care of you."

"And when I'm well . . . ?" His eyes bore into her like bullets.

She smiled. "When you're well," she whispered, "I'm going to make love to you until you lose your mind."

His smile was one of pure, animal desire—tempered by his recent accident, of course. "God, I hope so," he breathed. "But then, Nadia?"

"I'll stay with you," she murmured. "Forever."

"I don't want you to stay out of pity."

"That's good," she countered. "Because I'm not."

He cleared his throat. She was about to ring the nurse for some water or apple juice for him, when he surprised her by reaching out, holding her hand.

"The contract . . ." he said. "Alexis is dead. That means I'm free. *We're* free."

She felt the word and its meaning sink in. *Free.*

"Will you marry me?"

She blinked. She hadn't expected that. His eyes looked hopeful—even as she could feel the tension in his hand, hear it in his voice.

"Yes," she said, and he let out a deep breath. "I expect to have a job of some sort," she quickly added. "I want to be more independent. I'll have my own life."

He frowned at this, opening his mouth as if to protest.

She cut him off with a quelling look. "You'll just have to trust me."

He nodded, grinning slowly. "I may get a little crazy at times, because it's hard for me. I've been this way for a long time. But I promise to try."

She smiled. "Then you'll start to get more of a life, too. You'll find something you like doing. And we'll both make love and have a life together."

He nodded. "I can live with that."

Chapter Fifteen

Jelena walked into Phillipe's house. He was having a party; he'd specifically invited her. She wore a daring dress, midnight blue, tailored to accentuate her body. People noticed; she could feel their gazes follow her as she walked steadily down his familiar hallway. He was holding court in his office, she noticed. When he saw her, he stood up, making a beeline straight for her.

"Jelena," he said, kissing both cheeks, European style. His eyes gleamed. "I'm so glad you could make it. I understand you've been quite busy lately."

She didn't blush. She shrugged. "It's been hectic."

He knew, she realized. About Alexis. About everything.

He put a familiar arm around her waist. If Henry could see her now, she thought bitterly.

Screw Henry.

"Why don't we talk somewhere a little more private?" Phillipe said, guiding her away from the throng of guests. He lead her back to his bedroom, closing the door on the party noises beyond. "You look phenomenal."

"Do I?"

"Yes." He gave her a frank appraisal, his gaze sweeping from her head down to her heels, slowing at her breasts and hips. "Power looks good on you."

She shrugged again. *It might look good, but it felt terrible.*

He leaned in to kiss her, and she turned her face away. He pulled back, surveying her. "What's wrong?"

"I don't need you anymore," she said simply. "I realize now I never did."

He looked offended. "Some way to treat your mentor."

"You never taught me anything," she pointed out. "You liked to think you're powerful, but you're just a penny-ante mindfucker who likes to think he's a guru."

His back stiffened. Then, slowly, he grinned. "Damn," he breathed. "You *are* amazing."

She scowled at him, stepping away when he reached for her. "I'm not playing hard to get, you idiot," she said. "I'm saying: leave me alone. I don't want to sleep with you. I don't even want to touch you."

His face went pale, then flushed red. "Then why, exactly, are you here?"

She froze.

Why are *you here?*

Before she could contemplate an answer, April walked

in. She had her hair up in a sophisticated upsweep, and was wearing a demure black cocktail dress. When she saw Jelena, she paused, her expression softening. "Mrs. Granville," she murmured.

Jelena's mouth went dry.

"Phillipe," she said. "You weren't completely useless."

"Oh, really?" he said caustically. "Where did I provide some small assistance, if I might ask?"

She walked up to April, then kissed her softly on the lips. April leaned in, sighing softly.

Jelena turned back to Phillipe. "You've got one hell of an assistant," she said. "I think I'll keep her."

"You're *what*?" Phillipe goggled. "You can't . . . she—"

"I quit," April said, without even looking at him. Jelena smiled warmly at her, feeling some of the awful numbness and confusion start to retreat. April hooked her arm in Jelena's. "I think we're done here, don't you?"

Jelena nodded. Then she walked with April back to her car. They drove to April's apartment—since the incident with Nadia, Jelena hadn't wanted to step into her large, empty mansion.

"I feel so lost," Jelena admitted as April poured her a glass of wine. "I thought I was doing the right thing, every step of the way. I thought I was correcting the damage." She winced, thinking of Robert, Phillipe, Alexis. The brothel. She shuddered. "The things I did . . ."

April smoothed Jelena's hair. "You did what you thought was best," she said softly. "It's over now. You can make new choices."

Jelena nodded. She still felt . . . raw. Confused. She needed someone to be there for her. Someone to help her cleanse this terrible sense of doubt and wrongness.

April must have sensed it. When Jelena finished her glass, April took it, setting it aside the way she had that first night they were together, at Phillipe's house. Then she tugged Jelena to her feet. She unzipped the midnight blue dress, turning to let Jelena undo her black one. The sounds of silk swishing to the floor were the only soft noises for a long moment, as they stood in lingerie, inches from each other. Waiting expectantly.

Jelena bridged the gap first, reaching out slowly, need coursing through her. She cupped April's breasts, stroking the petal-soft skin over the demi-cups of her bra. April smiled, stroking her shoulders. They kissed, quick, light brushes of lip against lip.

With a soft sound of desire, Jelena pressed her body against April's, feeling her nipples brush against April's erect ones. April wound her arms around Jelena's waist as Jelena buried her hands in April's hair, freeing it from its constraining style. Their breathing turned quicker, more uneven, and the kiss deepened. Jelena felt April's tongue rub against hers, causing her to go wet in a rush.

She reached down, her fingers moving past April's panties and nudging across the silken soft flesh of her shaved pussy. April let out a low squeal of delight, parting her legs slightly, giving her better access. She was already slick, Jelena noticed, and her stomach knotted pleasurably in anticipation. She moved April to the couch, not wanting to go all the way to the bedroom. She sucked on April's breast through the lace of the bra, every sound of April's arousal fanning the flames of her own desire.

The heat felt cleansing. The need, overpowering.

April took off her bra, and Jelena followed suit. Both shimmied out of their panties, laughing as they did, a free, happy sound. Then they were kissing again, and all laughter stopped. They stretched out on the narrow couch, so close together they took up no room. April pressed her leg between Jelena's parted thighs, and Jelena ground her pussy against it, needing more friction, more contact. "I want you," she murmured, rubbing her breasts against the redhead's and gasping at how the slight, sensitive contact sent shockwaves through her sexual system.

"Mmmm," April responded, parting the folds of her labia, and then doing the same with Jelena. When clit touched clit, Jelena cried out at the unexpected pleasure. She sat up, unconsciously breaking the contact. Frustrated, she tried again.

"Wait," April said, sitting up as well. They shifted, one leg overlapping the other, until they scissored together, their clits in constant contact, rubbing against each other. They faced each other, their hips gyrating in time as they ground against each other, the delicious conflagration of sensation searing through Jelena like nothing she'd ever felt before. She couldn't think. She could only feel.

She kissed April deeply, holding her as their hips moved in more frantic, reckless rhythm. Their stomachs made soft slapping noises. Their breathing, high pitched. She tore her mouth away, holding tightly, her hips lifting off the couch as she moved closer, closer . . .

The orgasm spread through her like wildfire, and she let out a long, shuddering cry. April trembled against her, and the responding wetness told her that they'd both orgasmed at the same time.

They held each other for a long time. "I never knew it could be like this," Jelena said, baffled but happy.

"You know what the best part is?"

Jelena looked over at April. "This?"

"Well, yes," April said, and she looked girlish and happy and mischievous. "What I was going to say, though, is that men need time to recover."

She leaned down, suckling first one breast, then the other. Jelena gasped in surprise.

"Women don't," April said.

They made it to the bedroom. This time, needing to feel something inside her, April brought out her box of toys. Though Jelena giggled at the bright neon pink piece of silicon, she wasn't laughing when April went down on her, sucking on her clit, rubbing the two-headed dildo against her sensitive pussy entrance. They repeated their previous position, only now, they both were penetrated. The feel of something thick inside her, plus April's skillful ministrations with a tiny vibrator touching both their joined clits, made Jelena come with the force of a nuclear bomb.

Then there was the shower. They clung to each other, one leg hooked over the other's hip, the peach-scented soap slick and smooth between their naked bodies. They shivered under the forceful hot spray, moaning and arching and rubbing against each other, crying out with completion as April's hand moved to guide and caress their twin triangular bumps.

They didn't sleep. When the grayish light of dawn finally crept through the window, Jelena had lost count of the times she had orgasmed. She felt deliciously drained, outrageously exhausted. She curled up with April in the bed, twisted in the chaotic sheets. They kissed passionately.

"I don't know where this is going," Jelena said. "But I like it."

"Don't worry," April said, as Jelena drifted off to sleep. "We'll figure it out together."

Six months later

"I'd forgotten how great it feels to be free," Dominic said, stretching out on the bed of the private jet.

Nadia smiled. For the past two months, they'd traveled around the world—London, Paris, Madrid. Even Australia. "I'll be glad to get home, though."

"I know," he agreed. "I miss Max."

She laughed ruefully. "Me too." As claustrophobic as it had felt, she missed simply being closed off from the world with Dominic. Living with him, enjoying each other. Having a simple life, just the two of them.

"Everything okay with your family?"

She shrugged. "Father went to jail."

Dominic's eyebrow went up.

"Porsche," she said. "Vintage."

"Ah." Dominic's expression was completely blank. "How are Deidre and the baby?"

"They're doing fine. Jelena's helping them."

"I will, too."

She sent him a grateful look, holding his hand. "I wish he could have straightened out," she said wistfully. "But . . ."

"We all do what we think is best." Dominic took a deep breath. "On a brighter note: I spoke with a few plastic surgeons. They think that they can reverse some of the damage."

"Oh?"

"No promises," Dominic said carefully. "No guarantees. But at least I won't look quite so . . ."

Nadia frowned. "So what?"

Dominic shrugged. "You know. Hideous."

The casual-sounding word was anything but. She held him, looking at him fiercely.

"You don't look hideous," she said, punctuating each word with a kiss. "If you want to try it, for you, that's fine. But I still love you. Whatever you look like."

He sighed, and she realized he'd been tense about his announcement. Yet another reason she loved him.

He nuzzled her neck, and she stretched out against his magnificent hard body. "I definitely miss you wandering around naked all day," he complained, unbuttoning her dress and easing it off her body.

She thrilled at his touch, her nipples tightening. She helped him take off his shirt, then undid his pants, freeing his large, already erect cock from its constraints. "You know what I miss?" she teased, nudging his pants off. "That table."

His eyes glowed. "We'll just have to make do until then, won't we?"

"Actually," she said, "I thought we might change it up a bit."

"I'm game."

She swallowed hard. She'd been contemplating this for a long time, too. Now, at forty thousand feet, locked in their private bedroom compartment, she hoped it was the right time.

"I think maybe we should switch roles."

His smile faded. "You mean . . . blindfold me? Tie me up?"

She nodded.

He hedged, a look of panic crossing his features. "I'm not sure . . ." Then he took a deep breath, kissing her. "But I trust you." He said it firmly, with determination.

She dashed to her carryon, where she'd brought the silk scarves. She tied one around his head, then anchored his wrists and ankles to the bed as best she could. At least she knew he shouldn't feel too constrained. The wispy material looked like it could barely contain him.

He was breathing quickly, more shallow, and she knew it was probably equal parts fear at being vulnerable, and the sensual excitement. She felt a tremor of pleasure, as well as a deep desire to ensure his experience was pleasurable.

She started with slow, long kisses, teasing him with it, pulling out of his reach. Then she traced a swirling pattern with her tongue, dipping into his collarbone, brushing against one hard masculine nipple. He let out a low groan of appreciation, and she felt heartened. When she moved across the hard, rippling planes of his abdomen, his groan grew louder, and his cock tugged. She could see the gleaming bead of wetness, there at the tip. She licked it off, tasting the minute salty drop.

His low moan echoed in the cabin, and his hips lifted off the bed.

"Not yet," she said, then took as much of him as she could into her mouth. She sighed in pleasure around his cock, suckling it, rubbing her tongue along the velvety soft mushroom cap, gently exploring the aperture at the top, stroking along the heavily pulsing vein. She stroked her hands on the shaft that she couldn't accommodate, slick with the wetness of her mouth. His hips rose in time with her licks, and his breathing was harsh and staccato.

She pulled back, and he made a noise of protest. "Not too fast," she said playfully, letting him cool down. Just sucking on him had made her grow wet. She cradled his cock between her breasts, massaging it, rubbing the head down the valley of her breastbone.

Then she straddled him, lowering herself by inches on his rock-hard shaft. She moaned herself as she felt him filling her.

He struggled against the bonds, and suddenly she wondered if she were doing it wrong. She laughed as the loud sound of material tearing filled the air. His arms were around her, and he was sitting up, kissing her, pulling her tight against him. Burying himself fully inside her.

"Shit," he muttered, and she pulled off his blindfold. He looked contrite—and hot.

"We'll keep working on it when we get home," she said, and then wrapped her legs around his waist, rocking against him, crushing her breasts against his chest. He pumped inside of her, lifting and lowering her on his erection with his strong arms. She'd never get enough of him. She whimpered, moving faster, rubbing her clit against his shaft, shifting and rolling so his cock brushed against the high, hard spot deep inside her pussy. The combined efforts triggered an orgasm like a shotgun blast, and she clenched around him, her cunt milking him until he came with a low shout.

When it was over, he kissed her, tenderly, pushing her sweaty bangs out of her face. "You are my home," he whispered.

She held him tight.

"Forever," she breathed. And gave herself over to pleasure.

CATHY YARDLEY has been entranced by fairy tales since she was three years old. Now, she spends her time weaving those fairy tales into modern retellings that keep the magic, romance, and twisted beauty in entirely contemporary settings and storylines. When not writing, Cathy spends time with her husband and son at home in southern California.